The Chalet Girls in Camp

The Chalet School series by Elinor M. Brent-Dyer

Above is a complete list of Chalet School titles though only those set in bold type are available in Armada paperbacks. Unfortunately we cannot keep all these titles in print simultaneously but an up-to-date stocklist can be sent on request.

Elinor M. Brent-Dyer

The Chalet
Girls in Camp

Armada

First published in the U.K. in 1930 by
W. & R. Chambers Ltd, London and Edinburgh
This edition was first published in Armada in 1969 by
Fontana Paperbacks,
8 Grafton Street, London W1X 3LA

Armada is an imprint of Fontana Paperbacks,
part of the Collins Publishing Group

This impression 1986

© W. & R. Chambers 1930

Printed in Great Britain by
William Collins Sons & Co. Ltd, Glasgow

CHAPTER I

HER ROYAL HIGHNESS the Princess Elisaveta Margherita, Crown Princess of Belsornia, sat on a grass bank and sang lustily one of the old English folk-songs. Anything less like the traditional princess it would have been hard to imagine. She wore a frock which had begun the day as a fresh pink linen, but which now looked only fit for the rag-bag, since she had torn it across the front of the skirt, and it was stained with blue-berry juice from throat to hem. Her arms and legs were brown as a gipsy's, and a scratch adorned her small, freckled nose. Her hair was scattered wildly over her shoulders, and she was engaged in undoing a knot in her hair-ribbon with fingers that would have been the better for a good scrubbing. Above her, sat her great friend, Joey Bettany, together with 'the Robin,' as Joey's small adopted sister was affectionately known; Juliet Carrick, a ward of Jo's elder sister, Madge Russell; and Grizel Cochrane. The last named, once a pupil of the Chalet School which Mrs. Russell had founded at the Tiernsee nearly five years previously, had now returned to be a mistress in the annexe the authorities were establishing at the Sonnalpe for delicate children.

'You're a sight to behold, 'Veta,' said Jo as the song came to a close.

The Princess looked up, the obstinate knot between her teeth. 'Well, you aren't much better!' was her reasonable retort.

'I dare say! But I'm not a princess—I'm only a com-moner.'

'You're a head-girl!'

'This is holiday-time,' declared Jo, clasping slender hands round her knee and watching her friend's struggles with interest. 'You know, that ribbon will never be fit for anything now. It's more like a piece of chewed string than anything else.'

The Princess removed it from her mouth and looked at it doubtfully. "It's the last I have here."

Juliet looked up at this. 'The *last*? Elisaveta Arnsonira! Do you mean to say that you've gone through six hair-ribbons in three weeks?'

'It looks like it,' said the Princess ruefully. '*I* don't know how it is that ribbons and handkerchiefs and stockings never seem to last here as they do at home.'

'If that's all that's puzzling you, I can easily answer it,' said Jo, with a chuckle. 'You don't romp about there as you do here. Just as well, too, or I don't believe any finances would stand the strain!'

Elisaveta glanced down at her frock. 'You needn't remind me of that! Madame will be sure to make me mend it—she always does! And, at any rate, your own is as bad. Just look at that beautiful triangular rip in your skirt!'

Jo sighed heavily. 'Madge is too conscientious—that's her trouble,' she said.

'But, Joey, I will help you to mend it,' put in the ten-year-old Robin eagerly. 'I can sew very neatly now— Tante Marguérite says so.'

Joey smiled tenderly down at her. 'You can, my treasure! But I'm not going to let you tackle *my* mending as well as your own.—It's no use, 'Veta,' she went on to the Princess. 'That rag you call a hair-ribbon will never be any better. You might as well tie up your hair with a shoe-lace at once. Come along home, and we'll tidy up. Isn't Madge expecting people to tea, by the way?'

'She said something about it,' agreed Juliet, as she rose to her feet and pulled up the Robin. 'It might be as well if we all changed. Robin isn't so bad, and Grizel and I are *whole*, at least; but there's no denying our frocks have seen better days. And we ought to put on stockings, too, I think. Madame didn't say whom she expected; for all we know, it might be the Prince of Wales—or the nearest dust-cart man. So we'd better be prepared for the worst.'

The Princess Elisaveta giggled. 'What a come down!

And what a choice! Very well, Juliet; we'll come. I suppose we ought to change. But stockings!'

'Never mind,' Jo comforted her, as they pulled lazy Grizel to her feet, and began to stroll slowly over the grass in the direction of 'Die Rosen,' the home of Dr and Mrs Russell, where all five were living. 'Camp will be coming off soon, and so long as we are decent for parade, it doesn't matter what we look like during the rest of the day.'

'It seems too splendid to think that I'm really going to camp with you all,' said the Princess, with a little skip of pure joy. 'Wasn't Dr Tracy a dear to say it was the very thing I needed?'

'Rather!' said Joey. 'But you know, 'Veta, you don't look the same girl who came here a fortnight ago.'

'I should think she doesn't!' laughed Grizel. 'She was respectable, clean, and tidy——'

'And looked as if she had been to the wash and the colours had run,' supplemented Jo cheerfully. 'Really, 'Veta, you looked like an underdone loaf of white bread.'

With which remarkable simile, they reached the garden gate, where they were met by Mrs Russell, Jo's sister, who eyed the disreputable-looking party with horror. 'Children!' she exclaimed. 'What in the world have you been doing? You look like a set of tramps!'

'Gathering *Blaubeeren,*' explained Jo, showing her laden basket. 'Heaps here for both jelly and jam, to say nothing of pies.'

'Still—*was* there any need for you to tear yourselves to rags like this?'

'Madame, *we're* comparatively decent!' protested Grizel, including Juliet with a wave of her hand. 'At least we're whole.'

'And having said that, you've said all,' declared Madge Russell. 'Even my Robin looks more like gipsy than a member of the Chalet School. Well, you must hurry and change, all of you. My visitors will be here before long —Jem saw them coming up the path half an hour ago, so they can't be much longer now. Run along, all of you!'

Jo hung back a moment, as the others set off to the

house. 'Madge, who are they? You're making an awful fuss about them.'

'If you wait, you'll see,' said her sister, running her fingers through the fine black hair that was tousled till Jo's head looked like a floor-mop. 'Hurry up, Joey-Baba, and make yourself presentable. You're anything *but* at present.'

Jo frowned, then shrugged her shoulders, and ran after the others, catching them up at the front-door. They passed in, and along the cool hall, where bowls and jars of flowers lent their delicate perfume to the coolness and darkness; then on, upstairs to the corridor known as 'the children's corridor'; there they all separated, the Robin trotting off to the nursery to seek Rosa, the nurse, while Juliet and Grizel turned into the first door, and Jo and Elisaveta made for one at the end.

'Do you know who it is?' asked the Princess, as she struggled out of her frock. 'I saw you stop to ask Madame.'

'She won't say,' laughed Jo, tossing her own dress into the soiled-linen basket. 'Look here, 'Veta, put that rag in here, and don't leave it on the floor for everyone to see! You *are* an untidy kid—worse than I am! Aliette must be thankful for a holiday from you!'

The Princess picked up her frock and dumped it in on top of Jo's. 'If you think Aliette picks up after me, you're mistaken,' she informed her friend. 'I have to be tidy at home, I can tell you.'

'Well, don't get into bad ways here,' said Jo, who was now seated on the side of her bed, pulling on her stockings. 'It won't do in camp, I can tell you *that*. We camped a good many week-ends last term, you know, and you've got to have the whole place as neat—as—as—a hospital,' she added, as she glanced out of the side window, and caught a glimpse of the huge sanatorium which was the reason for the existence of the village on the Sonnalpe.

'Are you going to change all through?' asked the Princess, conveniently ignoring the last part of the speech.

'Just as well. It feels fresher, anyway.'

'All right, then. What frock, do you think?'

'Better put on white—or no; you're so brown! Put on

8

that pretty yellow thing you have there. Then your colour mayn't show so badly,' advised Jo.

Elisaveta nodded, and took the frock out of the wardrobe, and for the next few minutes the pair were too busy to chatter. Jo made a dive for the bathroom, but Juliet was before her, and she had to wait till the latter had finished. Grizel and Elisaveta had to hurry over their washing, but at length all four were ready, and looking very different people from the untidy group who had come home twenty minutes before. Elisaveta, in the yellow muslin, with her hair brushed and combed and fastened back by a clasp, looked more like her rank. Jo, in soft blue, with the golliwog mop reduced to order, made a very good example of a head-girl; while the elder two were a pair that any head-mistress might have been proud to introduce as members of her staff.

Finally the Robin, now a rosebud in her pink frock, came running to seek them, and they all went down to the garden where Mrs Russell was sitting in a comfortable *chaise-longue*, while her small son crawled about on the dry brownish grass at her feet, and Peggy and Rix, her little nephew and niece, sat in another corner, building a tower with their bricks.

Another person was there—a slender girl of fourteen, with bobbed fair hair and keen grey eyes. She was paler than the others, and was strapped into an invalid chair, which was partly raised at the back. This was Stacie Benson, a member of the School, who had injured her spine at the end of the last Easter term, and who was still unable to walk. Indeed, the elder people had been having a good deal of anxiety about her. At first she had seemed to progress with great rapidity; but during the past three weeks all progress had ceased, and she had even gone back a little, so that it had been deemed wiser to lower the back of the chair again, in order to help the bruised and strained muscles to strengthen. She knew nothing of the worries of the elders, and thought the reason for her tiredness when she had 'sat up' for any length of time was just the result of the very hot weather. They hoped that she need never know, and saw to it that none of the other girls suspected that there was anything wrong. But Dr

Russell had written a very long letter to her aunt and guardian at the beginning of the previous week, and Mrs Trevannion had written to say that she and her husband hoped to come to the Sonnalpe in a fortnight's time.

Stacie looked up with a smile as the little bevy of girls joined them. 'Hullo, you people! Get many *Blaubeeren*?' she asked.

'Loads,' said Jo. 'Madge, when are these visitors of yours coming? Will they be long? 'Cos I'm hungry; I want my tea.'

'I can hear their voices now,' said her sister, as she picked up her son and got up to go and welcome her guests.. 'Elisaveta, run to the gate and open it, dear.'

The Princess went off to do as she was told. The next minute she had flung it open and was racing down the road with a cry of 'Daddy!'

'The King?' gasped Joey, tugging her skirts straight. 'Why ever didn't you tell us? Oh, and 'Veta's got a most awful scratch on her nose!'

'I don't suppose the King will mind that,' smiled Madge. 'He will only look at her roses and——'

'And freckles!' suggested Grizel. 'She has plenty of *them*, anyhow.'

'So have you,' said the Robin.

It was true, but Grizel hated any mention of the fact. Usually, she was careful to avoid exposing her face to the sun; but the *Blaubeeren* gathering had made her forget her caution, and her pretty nose was as plentifully besprinkled with 'sun-kisses' as Elisaveta's. She flushed, and opened her lips to say something sharp; but, fortunately, the gate opened again, and the Princess, her hands clasped round the arm of a tall, handsome man, came in, chattering like a magpie. 'Madame, it's Daddy!' she cried, as she towed him across the lawn to receive the curtseys of the others. 'Oh, what a lovely surprise!'

'I am glad you could come, Sire,' said Madge, with a smile, as the party found seats for itself, once the greetings were over. 'I am afraid Elisaveta has not improved herself with that scratch——'

'It only happened to-day,' said the Princess. 'It's all

right, Madame. Jo had iodine with her, and she rubbed some in at once.'

The King laughed. 'At least, she looks well and strong again,' he said. 'I can see that she is having all the open-air treatment advocated by our good Dr Tracy.'

'Where *is* Dr Tracy?' asked Mrs Russell. 'My husband saw him with you.'

'Dr Russell carried him off to the sanatorium to show him the new violet-ray installation,' said the King. 'I suppose they will come along when they have exhausted all its possibilities. And is this your boy? What a fine, healthy little fellow he looks! And Joey is longer than ever!—When are you going to stop growing, Joey?'

'Not yet, I hope,' said Joey cheerfully. 'I'm only *just* taller than Madge, and I'd like to reach to Juliet before I'm finished.'

The King looked across at the tall fair girl opposite him, and smiled. 'I doubt if that will happen. Juliet was a very tall girl when she was your age. And you're built on a smaller scale.'

'My parents were both tall,' said Juliet. 'Madame once told me, Jo, that your mother was very small. You may be like her.'

'Jo isn't small, even now,' said Mrs Russell. 'But I think his Majesty is right, Joey, and you won't reach Juliet's inches. You're long enough, anyway, for you. I object to having a sister a head or so above me!'

'Oh well, never mind that,' said the Princess, who thought she had been left out of the conversation quite long enough. 'Let us talk of the camp next week.'

The King laughed pleasantly. 'That is so important to you, little daughter, is it not?' he said, pulling one of her long brown curls as he spoke. 'She looks well, Madame —better even than I had hoped she might. It speaks well for your care.'

Madge smiled. 'Better for our fresh air and sunshine, Sire,' she replied. 'The girls are out in it all day long. I am afraid Elisaveta has developed a good many freckles, and a coat of tan that will make Aliette hold up her hands in horror——'

'I like her best so,' he said, with a glance at the child's

11

face. 'She was a very white flower when she left me. But now she looks as I like to see her. Does Doctor Jem think it well for her to go with the others? It is difficult for her to join in a camp in Belsornia. But here, if the doctors will only consent, it is possible and desirable.'

'Jem says it is the best thing for her,' said Jo, as she contemplated her friend thoughtfully. 'She's fatter than she was, your Majesty—don't you think so?'

Before anyone could reply, the Princess had sprung up and hurled herself bodily on Jo, who, unprepared for the shock, rolled over, shrieking at the top of her voice. At once the somewhat prim and formal party changed its character and developed into a scrimmage, from which the two authors emerged untidy, but cheerful.

By this time Rosa, the children's nurse, had brought out Rix and Peggy Bettany, whose father, Madge Russell's twin brother, worked in the forest department in India. When father and mother had returned to India they had taken with them Baby Biddy, their youngest child. But the three-year-old twins had been left in the charge of 'Auntie Madge,' since they throve in the pure mountain air, and India was not good for them. They had never before met the King, but shyness was not among their many virtues and vices, and they made for their elder aunt with shouts of joy.

'Tantie Guito!' cried Rix, using the name Robin often called the gentle woman who had taken the place of her mother, 'Tantie Guita, I want to go to camp too!'

'Me as well,' pleaded Peggy, a fair little maid with serious blue eyes under a mop of silky, fair curls. 'Me as well, please, Tantie!'

Madge set the pair on their feet and directed them to the guest. 'Twins, we have a visitor! Go and say "How-do-you-do" to his Majesty.'

'What's zat?' asked Rix, who possessed an inquiring mind.

'It's my daddy,' said the Princess.

'No—a ma-zes-tee?' explained the small boy, pushing back the black hair that clustered in thick curls about his head.

'He's a king—that's what he's called,' said Jo. 'Go on, Peggy; where are your manners, children?'

The twins advanced, hand-in-hand, and the King smiled, for they were a charming pair; Rix being as dark as Peggy was fair, with his Aunt Madge's deep brown eyes, set in a little brown face which was mainly characterised by a chin startlingly square in such a baby. 'How-do-you-do?' they both said together; and then, as he held out his hands to them, they grabbed them. In a moment his Majesty had Peggy on his knee, while Rix leaned against him, asking excitedly, 'Why are you "Ma-zes-tee?"'

'Because I am a king,' said the King, with a smile.

'Where's ve c'own, ven?' demanded Peggy.

'I left it at home. It's too heavy to carry about with me.'

The twins considered this. 'Don't you wear it always?' asked Rix at length.

'No; it would be an awful nuisance,' returned the King as seriously as the boy had asked the question.

'Why?'

Jo rushed in. 'For goodness' sake don't start why-ing, Rix!—Don't let him, Sire. Once he begins, he never knows when to leave off.'

The King put her aside gently. 'It's a sensible question, Jo. He's entitled to a sensible answer if I can give it.—Listen, Rix! How would you like to wear your hat always—wherever you went?'

'I s'ouldn't,' said Rix, having considered this.

'Then you can understand that I don't want to wear my crown always. It is far heavier than my hat and not so comfortable. So I never wear it unless I must. I don't think any king does nowadays.'

'I see!' Rix was quite content with this answer, and presently ran off with his twin to see Rosa and his small cousin, David Russell—the latter a delightful person of fifteen months old, and one who seemed very willing to be ordered about by such a grown-up person as Rix. The Robin went with them, for she kept a motherly eye on Peggy, and often interfered when Master Rix's games seemed likely to involve his gentle sister in trouble.

The King looked after them with a smile. 'What a fine boy, Mrs Russell! Is he like his father? He has a strong resemblance to you.'

'Dick is fair,' said Madge, 'but there is a family likeness, of course. It's the joke of the family that Rix really might be my own son rather than my nephew. He's a handful!'

'All the better,' said the King. 'He ought to make a fine fellow later. The will is there, to judge by his chin.'

'He's as obstinate as—as——' Jo paused, hunting for a simile.

'As yourself, Joey,' said her sister calmly. 'Rix may be like me in face; but in character, he is you over again.'

'Me!' gasped Joey, looking outraged. 'I never flew into the tempers he does. I'm sure.'

'No; he gets that from Mollie's father, so she says. But you were just the same for mischief and curiosity when you were *his* age.'

'They're both dears,' said the Princess. 'But never mind about that; I want to talk about camp.—I *can* go just like the others, can't I, Daddy?'

'Yes, you may,' he said.

Elisaveta clapped her hands, and danced wildly around, crying ecstatically, 'Oh, it's too glorious!'

'Suppose you all go and discuss the matter, and leave me to have a sensible chat with his Majesty?' suggested Madge.

'A good idea,' he said. 'Elisaveta, take yourself off with these scaramouche friends of yours, and while you decide how many pairs of stockings and sheets you must take, I will talk it all over with Madame.—Run, you people!'

The girls got up, Joey taking Stacie's chair and pushing it along, so that she could join in the chatter, even though camp was not to be for her.

Mrs Russell and the King watched them disappear round a bend in the path. 'Elisaveta is wildly excited at the prospect,' he said.

'I think they all are,' said Madge. 'Of course, our girls have been camping out at intervals during the term. But this will be the first long camp, and they are to have it to themselves. I am so glad you are letting the Princess go with them.'

'Tracy says it is the best thing possible for her,' he said absently. There was a moment's silence; then, just as Madge was about to speak, he turned to her again. 'Madame, forgive me, and believe it is only deep friendship that makes me speak of it. It is some time—more than a year—since I saw Jo. Has she been ill? She looks very delicate to me.'

CHAPTER II

JOEY

"VERY delicate?—Joey?—Why, Sire, what do you mean?' Madge Russell's face, as she turned to the King, was white with apprehension, and her eyes were wide with panic.

He looked horrified at her appearance, and hastened to soften what he had said. 'You will forgive me, Madame, I had no wish to alarm you. But Joey is dear to all Belsornians for the way she risked her life in order to save Elisaveta from Cosimo, and—it may be that it is so long since I have seen her, and she has grown so much—but she has a frail look, to my eye.'

'She was very ill last autumn,' said Madge slowly.

'I know that. But this is many months later. Surely she has had time in which to recover from that illness.'

'We have had much trouble over the Robin this last term—and you know how Jo adores her.'

'What was that?' asked the King quickly. 'I had no idea—has she been ill too?'

'Not exactly that.' Madge had recovered herself a little, and the pink had returned to her cheeks. 'But you remember Jo wrote and told Elisaveta about the accident they had during the half-term week-end when Miss Wilson took some of the girls to Fulpmes? Well, that accident delayed them on the mountain-side, and the Robin, who was left at Fulpmes with one of the other girls, fretted terribly. The fretting told on her—you know how little extra strength she has—and, this term, Jem thought it advisable to keep her up here, so that she might recover. Unfortunately, certain symptoms began to develop which alarmed us all. They, happily, have proved to be only the outcome of her sudden growth. But for some time no one could say definitely what might happen. Jo knew, of course, and she worried terribly.'

'There is no further need to fear for the baby?' asked the King with interest, for he knew the Robin's story.

It was nearly five years since Madge Russell, then Madge Bettany, had brought the Robin to the Chalet School, a motherless baby of six. Her mother had died of tuberculosis, brought on by exposure during the war, and there was always the fear that the little girl had inherited the deadly disease along with the frailty of the dead mother. The doctors of the Sonnalpe sanatorium had watched the child closely all these years, and now, with the Robin almost eleven, they were beginning to hope that she would escape. But until the growing-years were past, there was always the danger, and this the King knew. He, like everybody else, was very fond of the little half-Polish girl, and the news Madge Russell was giving him caused a contraction in his throat. 'She will not have to fight against that, will she?' he asked, as Madge remained silent.

'They hope not. But it means that she must stay up here until she is at least eighteen,' replied Mrs Russell quietly. 'You have heard of our annexe, of course? She will be educated there, along with some of the others whom it will be as well to have under the immediate care of our doctors. But they all hope that the Robin will escape.'

'And Joey knew of this fear?'

'How could we keep it from her?' she asked. 'If—if the worst had happened, she would never have forgiven us for keeping her in ignorance, and she would have lost her trust in us. She had to know, Sire.'

'I see.' The King frowned; he was thinking deeply. 'Then you think that it has preyed on Jo's health?'

16

'It never struck me. I see her every day,' faltered Madge. 'She has never been robust, as you know. I—Oh, *Jem!*'

Dr Russell making a leisurely way across the grass looked up in amazement at his wife's exclamation. Then he hurried to her side. 'Madge! What's wrong with you?'

'The King——' began Madge.

'I am afraid I have been frightening your wife,' said the King, as he gripped the other man's hand. 'I felt worried over Joey——'

'Over Joey?' Jem Russell became suddenly wary. 'What's wrong with her?'

'She looked so—delicate to me.'

The doctor thought a moment. 'I noticed she was looking tired this morning.—Where is she, Madge?'

'In the grove, playing with the children,' said Madge.

He raised his voice in a shout of 'Joey!' and a long, melodious call came back, followed a moment later by Joey herself. She ran up to her brother-in-law, asking, 'What on earth do you want now?'

'What mischief are you all plotting?' Jem demanded, the while his experienced eyes were running over her, noting the purple smudges under her soft black eyes; the slight hollowness at temples and cheek-bones; and the indefinable air of fragility which he suddenly saw in her.

'Mischief? I'll thank you, Jem Russell, to remember that I'm rather big for mischief,' retorted Jo. 'We were playing with the kids, if you really want to know.'

'You look rather overdone,' he said. 'What have you been up to?'

'Nothing. It's just this heat,' said Jo. 'I love hot weather, but this beats everything. I shall be thankful to get away to camp, where it's cool. I couldn't sleep last night, I was so hot.'

'Why didn't you let me know?' he asked.

'What's the use? You couldn't do anything about it.'

'Oh yes, I could, you ungrateful monkey. I'm going to do something about it now. You people can all sleep out to-night. After *Kaffee*, you can get your hammocks slung under those trees—you and Grizel, and Juliet and Elisaveta, at any rate. You'll find it cool enough there.'

17

'Jem, you dear!' Joey flung herself on him with a rapturous hug.

'Joey! Drop it—it's too hot for embraces!' he protested.

She let him go with a laugh, and sped back to the others to tell them the delightful news.

The doctor turned to the King. 'Thank you very much, Sire. I'm afraid I haven't been keeping a close enough watch over Jo. The heat is pulling her down, but this will probably settle the not sleeping, and camp will put her all right.' He bent over to Madge. 'Don't worry, old lady. There's nothing radically wrong with Jo. She and the rest can camp out now, and they'll be off to camp next week. The Baumersee is higher even than this, so they'll be cool enough there. But you might cut down sweets and so on for the present. Plenty of fruit, plain biscuits, and lemon drinks. No meat or rich cakes. And I'll make up a cooling mixture for her, and for goodness' sake see that she *takes* it! I haven't forgotten what happened to the last mixture I gave her.'

'What was that?' asked the King curiously, as Jem sank down into a chair and mopped his brow.

Madge began to laugh. Her soft colour had returned, and the worry had left her face. 'Oh, only Jo was out of sorts for a few days, and Jem made up a prescription for her. There was some kind of powder in it, and the bottle had to be well shaken. It was a most unpleasant mixture, I must admit, for I tasted it. Jo found out, however, that, by judicious handling—in other words, by not shaking—it was possible to get a beverage that was not bad to take. The monkey did it, and went through two bottles without them doing much good. Then Jem instituted inquiries, and found out what had been happening. I don't fancy,' she added pensively, 'that Jo will play *that* particular trick again.'

The King raised his eyebrows, but Jem only shook his head and laughed, and Mrs Russell refused to say any more. *Kaffee*, which took the place of English afternoon-tea with them, appeared just then, and the children came back to the lawn, where his Majesty was pleased to see that his own small daughter had quite recovered the appetite she had lost before she had come to the Sonnalpe. Joey ate less, but she enjoyed what she ate, though she grumbled at the embargo Jem laid on sweet cakes. After tea, he refused sweets to them all, including even Juliet and Grizel in his dictum. 'The less you eat of that kind of thing the better while this hot weather lasts,' he said. 'Trot off, now, and get your hammocks rigged up.'

'Me, too,' pleaded the Robin. 'I can sleep in the grove too, can't I, Oncle Jem?'

'Yes,' he said. 'You must promise not to talk or chatter after you go to bed, of course. If you will do that, you may certainly sleep with the others.'

So it was arranged, and while Joey, Juliet, and Grizel put up the hammocks, Elisaveta went for a walk with her father, and Mrs Russell retired indoors to superintend bedtime for her own small son and the twins. The Robin was left in the charge of Stacia, who, very tired by this time, had been lowered to the level, in which position she perforce could do nothing. However, the small girl had a new book of fairy-tales, so she brought it, and Stacie, who had never heard any in her early childhood, and who now enjoyed them, all the more, perhaps, on that very account, lay and listened while the small girl read aloud to her the tale of Princess Lilamani and the Lapland sorcerer.

Bedtime came early for the school-girls, since Jem so decreed it, and Juliet and Grizel, tired out by the great heat, went off soon after them. Finally only the three 'grown-ups' were left in the big salon. Moths came fluttering through the open windows to flutter round the electric lamps, and the perfumes of the night poured into the quiet room.

'How many go to camp?' asked his Majesty.

'Thirty,' replied Madge. 'Miss Wilson, Miss Stewart, and Miss Nalder are going with them; and, of course, none of the very little ones will go. We made the Fourth form the limit. I believe the younger ones are very indignant about it,' she went on, 'but it is better so. Some of those middles—well, you know what middles are, Sire. I'm sure Elisaveta must have told you enough from her own two terms with us to enable you to realise that even three mistresses and most of the prefects will have their hands full.'

The King laughed. 'Oh, I can guess. Well, it is a splendid thing, and I am very glad for Elisaveta to have this chance. It would be difficult for her to camp out in Belsornia. I am afraid no Guider would care for the responsibility, and the camp would be surrounded by reporters at all hours. Here, of course, where she is just Elisaveta Arnsonira, and unknown, it is possible.'

A low humming of planes outside brought them to their feet, and the King said regretfully, 'Ah, here is Trevillion and my plane. I must go.'

'This is a short visit, Sire,' said Madge, as she laid her hand in his.

'Very short. But there is so much business that I am thankful I could get away, even for so short a time,' he replied.

Jem rang the bell, and presently his Majesty's bag was brought down and carried out to the plane, while Captain Trevillion, his equerry, chatted pleasantly with the Russells, and drained a glassful of fruit-juice drink before he put on his helmet and gloves again and climbed up into the pilot's seat in the aeroplane. The King followed, having run down to the hammocks to kiss his little daughter in her sleep. The engine roared into life again, and a few moments later they were far above the Sonnalpe, heading for Belsornia. Madge and Jem watched till the aeroplane was a mere speck in the starlit skies. Then they turned back to the house.

'I am thankful he came,' said Madge, as she watched her husband shut the windows in the salon. 'But he scared me horribly about Jo at first.'

'No need for that,' said the doctor. 'It's only the heat, and she'll soon recover at the Baumersee.'

CHAPTER III

THE START

THREE days had passed since the King's visit. The girls sat in the salon at breakfast, at which the Robin but not the babies was present. The meal was spent in arguing as to what should be the day's programme. Juliet wanted to walk round to the other side of the Alpe, and picnic there for the day. Grizel and Joey declared that a novel way of spending the day would be on the lake.

'We can go down as soon as we've finished *Frühstück*,' said Jo. 'We can get boats, and row about this morning. *Mittagessen* at the "Kron Prinz Karl," and then we can lie about in the pine-woods while it's hot, and row home after *Kaffee* at the "Stephanie."'

The Robin was charmed at the suggestion, but Mrs Russell shook her head. Jo might be much better for the sleeping out, but she tired easily, and her sister knew that the long pull up the mountain-side to the Sonnalpe after the day spent in rowing on the lake would wear her out. 'No, girls,' Mrs Russell objected. 'It's too much for such appallingly hot weather as we are having just now. You must content yourselves with less strenuous pastimes today.'

It was Dr Jem, as the girls called him, who settled the matter. 'You'll do none of the charming things you've planned,' he told them. 'Have any of you chanced to look to the south since you got up this morning?'

'The south? No—not specially. Why? Should we?' demanded Grizel.

'Well, if you take my advice, you'll go and fetch your beds in,' he said.

'As it happens, we fetched them in first thing this morning,' said Joey. 'But why the fuss? There isn't going to be a storm. Look at the sunshine!' she added protestingly.

'That's because this room faces east,' he said calmly. 'But I turned to the south when I left the sanatorium before *Frühstück* this morning, and——'

His sentence was finished for him by a low growl of thunder, and the entire party stampeded upstairs to the nursery, whose windows were above the tree-tops, and looked to the south. What they saw there appalled them. Rolling up against the heavens was a mass of black cloud, so heavy that it seemed literally to lie on the mountain-peaks. The edge of it was fringed with a livid white, which made the blackness all the more horrible, and, every now and then, blue lightning shot across it, rending it apart for a second.

'Oh!' gasped Joey, who was very impressionable.

'Pretty awful,' said Grizel. 'It's obvious there'll be neither picnic nor boating to-day. Even if the storm doesn't last long, everywhere will be soaked with the rain that the storm's going to bring.'

Whereupon a heavier crash of thunder than any that had gone before sent little Peggy to Juliet's side with a whimper, and the girls picked up the twins and bore them off downstairs. Mrs Russell took her baby and followed them to the salon, where Dr Jem was already shutting the windows against the coming of the rain.

It was not long delayed. With a mighty '*Crash!*' that nearly stunned them all, the storm broke on them, and lasted for five hours, circling the lake again and again. Madge, with David in her arms and the Robin pressed close to her side, sat by the empty stove. Juliet had Peggy cuddled up beside her, and Rix snuggled between Joey and Grizel. Elisaveta sat beside Stacie, one hand in hers, and they watched with awed eyes the battle between the mighty forces of Nature.

'Isn't it awful?' whispered the Princess once, clutching Stacie's fingers so tightly as to draw an anguished 'Ow!' from that young lady.

The storm lasted until after *Mittagessen*. After that, it drew off, and the sun came out again, shining on a fairy world, where every grass-blade and flower-petal was hung with gleaming drops, and the grass, so parched and brown only that morning, was transmuted into a sheet of living

22

green. The paths were rivers, and the lawn would be like a morass underfoot, so they were all forbidden to go out. The babies, worn out by the excitement of the storm, went off to bed, and slept till *Kaffee*. Juliet betook herself to her own room to write to her fiancé, who was in London at the moment. Grizel went with her—ostensibly to finish a book, actually to fall asleep on the light wicker lounge, and sleep as soundly as the babies in the night nursery. The Princess and Joey curled up together on Joey's bed, with the Robin between them, and Jo began to tell stories. But first the Robin drowsed off; then Elisaveta, nodding sleepily, observed Joey's voice becoming very foggy, and lifting her heavy eyes, saw that the storyteller was nearly 'over.' She stretched out, turned over on her side, and when Mrs Russell, startled at the quietness in the house, came up to see what they were all doing, she found them sleeping so sweetly, she hadn't the heart to waken them. She tucked them up with a rug, and left them to have their nap out.

'So there's *one* day simply thrown away!' said Joey, when she came downstairs later on, looking very shamefaced, but much refreshed by her sound sleep.

'Never mind. You'll have any amount of time for picnics and rowing when you get to camp,' said her sister. 'I'm sure you're all much better for a siesta now.'

The next day was Sunday, when everyone but the babies went to hear Mass in the little church behind the sanatorium. Usually there was a Protestant chaplain there, but Mr Eastley had taken three weeks' holiday to go home to see his wife's relatives and tell them what he could about her quiet death in the previous May, so the only service was in the little church dedicated to St Wenceslas. After it was over, the girls lounged about the garden till they were called in to *Mittagessen*.

In the afternoon some of them went down to see Frau Doktor Mensch and her little daughter, who lived at 'Das Pferd.' Gisela Mensch, in the days when she had been Gisela Marani, had been the first head-girl of the Chalet School, and they had all loved her dearly. She was still as sweet and thoughtful as she had been then, and Baby Natalie was a treasure. Staying with her brother and his young wife was Frieda Mensch, Joey's great chum and ally, and Gisela's own small sister, Maria, now a leggy school-girl of fourteen, with dark hair hanging in two thick plaits to her waist and a bright, vivid little face. Frieda, on the other hand, was of the fair, North German type, with long, fair plaits, sunny blue eyes, and skin of apple-blossom colouring. She and Jo, whose black locks and eyes were rather startling in conjunction with her pale skin, made a striking contrast, in character as in looks, for Frieda was gentle, quiet, rather shy, and the embodiment of her name—'Peace.' Jo, on the contrary, was quick, determined, with the 'gift of the gab' and a lively imagination which often got her into difficulties. It was, perhaps, the very unlikeness between them that made them so friendly. They were always happy together, and not one quarrel had ever marred their friendship.

Kaffee was taken with the Mensches, and then the entire party walked back to 'Die Rosen,' as it was getting near the Robin's bedtime. After the little ones had gone off, the others gathered round the piano and Frieda's harp, which her brother Gottfried had carried up for her, and they had music till it was time to separate for the night.

The next day was Monday, and they spent it in getting ready for their camp. Palliasse-covers were brought out and inspected, and pillows were packed into them, as well as changes of clothing, horn tumblers, enamelled plates, knives and forks and spoons, blankets, one or two books in case there should come rainy days, brushes and combs and sponges and soap, and all the hundred and one articles that would be necessary. The Guiders were to meet them all at Briesau, the little village in which the school was situated, at ten o'clock the next day, and from there they would take the boat down the lake to Scholastika, the village at its foot. There, they would find the two charabancs waiting for them which were to take them to the Baumersee, a beautiful lake, far up the western mountains, on whose shores their camp was to be.

Monday was a scramble, and everyone was thankful when it came to an end and they were all able to go to bed, happy in the knowledge that their packs had already gone to Briesau by lorry, and that they had only themselves and what they carried in their knapsacks to take there in the morning.

Tuesday found the Robin rather inclined to be tearful, for she was to be left behind. She was too frail and too precious to be trusted even to the tender care of the Guiders, and must make up her mind to do without her adored Jo for the fortnight. Luckily, she was a sunshiny little person as a rule; and, like so many continental children, she had been trained to the most absolute and unquestioning obedience. So she did her best to cheer up, and succeeded in sending them off with a smile, though the tears were still not far distant.

'Plucky kid!' said Grizel Cochrane approvingly, as she led the way down the winding mountain-path, alpenstock in hand. 'It's hard lines on her; but I suppose it's the only thing to do.'

'Absolutely,' replied Jo, who was following with the Princess, while Juliet and Frieda gave a helping hand to Maria. 'It's just as hard on Stacie, too. It must be horrid to have to lie there all day!'

'Worse than that—I should hate it!' said Grizel briefly.

'Stacie has been very brave about it,' said Frieda. 'She is so different from the Eustacia who came to us in January, that sometimes I wonder if she was not "magicked," as Jo calls it, on that day in the mountains when she hurt herself.'

Grizel laughed. 'Oh, Frieda Mensch! Don't say that you believe in witches at *your* age! Fairy-lore may be all very well for babies like the Robin; but for a girl of nearly seventeen it's a little absurd.'

Frieda coloured hotly, and Jo rushed to the rescue at once. '*Stop* being horrid and sneery, Grizel! How do you know there aren't any fairies? You don't know everything, though you *do* think you're so jolly clever and omniscient!'

Grizel opened her lips to reply. She and Jo had always squabbled more or less, for they were naturally antagonistic. However, before she could say anything, Juliet touched her arm, and she closed her mouth firmly. It would scarcely do to begin the fortnight's camp with a quarrel. Fortunately, at that moment they came to the stiffer part of the walk, and all were too busy negotiating the rocks and tree-roots to have breath to waste in argument. They soon got past this part, and the rest was easy enough, following the banks of a tiny stream that ran down the mountain-side to form a rill at the side of the road and empty itself finally into the lake.

At the foot of the mountain they were greeted with shouts which came from a little group of girls who were awaiting them there.

The Princess replied with a yell, and plunged forward. 'Margia—Giovanna—Evvy!' she cried. 'Oh, how nice to see you all again!—Lonny, you've grown heaps taller! —Vanna di Ricci! Where's your hair?'

'I have cut it off,' replied the last-named, a graceful Italian girl of Jo's age. 'It was so long and thick and hot.'

'I like it,' decided Elisaveta. 'Where's Amy, Margia?'

'Too young,' returned Margia, a bright-faced girl of fourteen, whose square chin and determined air gave the key to her character. 'It's awfully jolly having you back, 'Veta. Are you staying all the time?'

'Yes, of course! Isn't it splendid?' said the Princess, turning interested eyes on the rest of the group.

Jo proceeded to introduce them. ''Veta, these are Cornelia Flower, Elsie Carr, and Anne Seymour.—Girls, this is Elisaveta Arnsonira, who used to be at the Chalet School. She's at home with governesses and things now,' she added, with no more than her customary lucidity.

Elsie, a pretty, dark child of Margia's age, and Cornelia, a fair-haired American about a year younger, welcomed her rapturously. Anne Seymour nodded pleasantly, and then turned to the older girls. She was Fifth form, and expecting to be Sixth next term, and she felt rather grown-up in comparison with this leggy child of Margia's standing, as she thought. The Princess, with her floating curls tied neatly back from her face and her air of child-like candour did not look her fifteen years. Jo was amused at Anne, but said nothing. It was good for Elisaveta, she thought, to get this off-hand treatment sometimes. 'Most people bow down before her because she is who she is,' reflected the head-girl. 'It hasn't spoilt her yet, but you never know. Sha'n't tell anything about her to any of the girls who have come since she left.'

'Well, if you babes have finished rhapsodising on each other's necks, suppose we get on,' suggested Grizel. 'Come along, Juliet. We'll lead the way.'

They set off again, Grizel and Juliet leading, while the juniors came next, all chattering at the tops of their voices, and Joey, Frieda, and Anne brought up the rear. They soon came to the little landing-stage at Buchau, whence they were rowed across the lake by one of the boatmen who ply there for hire during the summer months. As they reached Briesau, the main village on the lakeside, they were received with a cheer, and the next moment they were surrounded by the rest who were going to the camp. The two seniors forgathered with the Guiders—Miss Wilson, Miss Nalder, and Miss Stewart. Jo and Frieda became the centre of a large group of people of their own age and standing in the School. Anne made one of a quartette who stood to one side, conversing quietly. Maria rushed straight into a cluster of folk who were mainly from the Third form. Margia dragged the Princess along to a ring of damsels among who she recognised old friends, and they all talked together, and all at once.

For a few moments the Guiders put up with it and exchanged greetings with the two old girls.

Then Miss Wilson, who, as captain, took the lead, blew her whistle. Silence at once prevailed, and she delivered her orders rapidly. 'Girls! Pick up your packs—two girls to each pack. Now then, to the boat, as quickly as you can. Up to the deck, and form your ranks, so that we can be sure no one is left behind.'

They seized the packs, and in a very few minutes all were arranged in neat ranks, only the Princess, Juliet, and Grizel standing to one side. Miss Wilson sent Elisaveta to Joey Bettany's patrol, and assigned Juliet and Grizel to the charge of Marie von Eschenau temporarily. Then, while she and Miss Stewart took roll-call, Miss Nalder counted the packs to see that all were there. It was early yet, so there were not many visitors about, and the captain of the boat knew them all, and was quite willing to delay a few minutes if it were necessary. It was not so, however, for all were there, and the packs were in order. The ropes were loosed, and, with a mighty puffing and fussing, the little steamer set off on its further journey by way of Geisalm and Seehof to Scholastika at the bottom end of the lake, where the motor charabancs were waiting to take the Guides to their camp.

CHAPTER IV

ON THE WAY

AT Scholastika, the village at the far end of the lake, the charabancs were waiting for the girls, and behind them was the lorry piled high with palliasse-covers filled with their requirements, tents, ground-sheets, and all the other paraphernalia needed for camping. A crowd of interested natives stood round, watching the Guides disembark and take their seats, and one or two visitors from the hotel by the water-side came out to see them off.

There were three charabancs. Miss Wilson took charge of one, with Grizel Cochrane to help her; Miss Stewart took the next, with Juliet Carrick as her companion; and little Miss Nalder, the Physical Training mistress, had control of the last, Joey Bettany and Frieda Mensch going with her. The packs were all piled into the last, since it had only ten girls and one mistress, while the others had twelve persons each. Then the foremost driver started his engine, and they set off.

For a little while they followed the road to Tiernkirche, famed for its lovely old church which the girls had often visited. There was a shop there, too, where it was possible to get beautiful examples of Tiernsee pottery. This was up a road that turned to the west before reaching the church, and up this road the charabancs ran.

'I've never been farther up here,' said Joey to Frieda, as they sat together in the back with Miss Nalder beside them and seven juniors, including Evadne Lannis and Cornelia Flower, in front. 'I've often wondered where it led to, and now I shall know. Good!'

'Where did you think it led?' asked Miss Nalder, with a smile.

'I didn't know. Roads are so fascinating I always think,' said Jo. 'You never know what you are going to see when you turn a corner. It may be some wonderful beauty—or it may be——'

'A pig-sty,' suggested Evadne, as Jo paused for a word.

Jo, who had been going to philosophise, was brought up with a jerk, and glared at the interrupter. 'Evvy, you really are the edge! *That* wasn't what I was going to say.'

'I'll bet it was just as good,' chuckled Elsie Carr, who was beside Cornelia—these three were inseparables; Margia Stevenson made up their quartette. On this occasion, however, Miss Wilson, with some idea of lessening Miss Nalder's burden, had taken Margia with her.

Jo began to frown, but changed her mind, and grinned. 'Trust you babes to spoil a good idea!' she said amiably.

The trio objected to being called babes, but as Jo might easily have been much more cutting, they held their tongues on the subject, and turned their attention to the scenery through which they were passing.

'I don't think much of this,' said Elsie, looking discontentedly at the farms, where people were hard at work in the fields with the hay-harvest. 'We can see this sort of thing any day at Briesau."

'Wait till we come to the mountains,' said Frieda, who knew the district. 'You will see wonderful scenery then.'

'You know the Baumersee, don't you, Frieda?' asked Evadne.

The Tirolean girl nodded. 'But yes! Ah, it is beautiful —*wunderchön*—*grossartig*! You will like it, Evadne. It lies among mountains, and is not blue like our Tiernsee, but silvery when the sun shines on it. When the rain comes, it is dark—dark as night. And tall trees grow close to the shore in one part, and in another there is sand— white sand.'

'It's round about the sandy part the camp is to be,' said

29

Jo. 'I heard Bill say so. I suppose there's grass above it. Do the trees come round there, Frieda?'

'There is a broad, grassy patch,' said Frieda. 'Then there are bushes, and behind them come the pines. It is a delightful place for a camp.'

'What about milk and butter?' demanded Cornelia, who liked her food. 'How do we manage about them?'

Frieda laughed. 'There are farms, of course. Not very near, perhaps; but not too far to walk.'

'Say, I hope Bill gets a good supply of butter to begin with, then,' returned lazy Evadne.

'What difference would that make?' demanded Jo. 'We'll have to get the milk every day, anyhow.'

'What happens when it's wet?' asked Elsie.

'*Are* you made of butter or sugar?' asked Miss Nalder, taking part in the conversation. 'If you are, Elsie, it's rather a pity you came to camp, isn't it?'

Elsie turned scarlet, and Joey smiled in a superior way. 'You'll like it all right when you get there, my child. Going errands when you're camping and going errands ordinarily are two very different things.'

'Well, I don't know how *you* know!' flashed Cornelia. 'You've never done any more camping than the rest of us have.'

'Common-sense,' said Jo airily. 'Oooh! Frieda Mensch! You never told us it would be like this!' With which remark she lapsed into silence.

The road between the flat harvest-fields had been passed, and now they were running through forest, where the tall pines made dark arches overhead and the air was sweet with the balmy, resinous smell of pine-needles. Every now and then the trees gave place to little glades, where the sun shone down, and the grass was enamelled with tiny, vivid wild-flowers, over which butterflies flitted, clad in myriad hues, and the bees hummed —though that they had to guess at, for the charabancs ran anything but quietly. Now and then tiny rills tore across the path under bridges made of stone or logs, and there was a soft rustling of the late summer breeze among the branches. There were few birds among the pines, but in the glades, other trees appeared, and they saw tiny, brown-feathered birds flying about, very busy on their own affairs.

The peace of the forest seemed to fall over the girls, even Elsie forgetting her indignation at Jo's superiority of manner. As for Jo and Frieda, they were lost in delight. Miss Nalder, watching their absorbed faces, was interested to see how still they sat. Frieda's blue eyes were full of dreams, but Jo's black ones glowed with the soft inward fire they always showed when she was deeply thrilled by anything. Elisaveta, who was sitting beside Evadne, was flushed with joy; and even the two little Americans, who were matter-of-fact children, felt the stillness and beauty of it. The other juniors—Greta Macdonald, Violet Allison, Lilli van Huysen (a Dutch girl), and Ruth Wynyard—were a quiet lot, Greta, Violet, and Lilli being inclined to shyness, while Ruth, who was a jolly tomboy, had yet thoroughly absorbed the majesty that robes a prefect, and held Joey, the head-girl, in some awe.

They left the forest ways presently, to run through a little village, of which the principal feature was the church, with its spire atop of a huge cupola, as so many of them are built in the Tirol. Both spire and cupola were newly gilded, and gleamed gaily in the sun. Little linty-locked children ran to the fences to stare at the three charabancs with their loads of merry girls, all in the Guide uniform, and to chatter interestedly about them among themselves. One or two of the children crossed their fingers at them, 'making the horns,' lest these strangely-dressed people should bring ill-luck to the village. The Guides are not widely known in this part of the world, and it is certain that the inhabitants of this tiny woodland cluster of cottages had never seen anything like them before.

'What on earth do they do that for?' asked Cornelia, who was rarely quiet for long.

'Make the horns, d'you mean?' replied Joey. 'That's to keep off ill-luck.'

'What? But how should *we* bring them ill-luck?' protested Evadne. 'I think it's jolly rude of them!'

'Do you really mean, Joey,' protested Miss Nalder,

'that the people here are like that—believe in the evil-eye and witchcraft?'

'Rather!' said Jo. 'Haven't you ever heard of the old madman that tried to carry off the Robin the winter Grizel was head-girl? No? Oh well, there isn't time to tell it now—it's a long story. But he did—Corney met him later.—Didn't you, Corney?—And Grizel and I went off after them with my St Bernard, Rufus, and brought the baby away. However, what I started out to say was that everyone round the lake thought he was a devil.'

'Really?' Miss Nalder seemed impressed.

'I should say they did,' said Evadne, taking up the tale. 'Why, they used to cross themselves when they mentioned him!'

'But—it's not the Middle Ages!' exclaimed the Games mistress.

'In some ways, Madame, it *is*,' said Frieda. 'Education has come here but slowly, and in these little, out-of-the-way villages, they have a firm belief in all sorts of—of——'

'Supernatural things,' Jo helped her out.

'Yes, that is the word.'

'It seems impossible!'

'It wouldn't have if you'd seen him,' said Cornelia. She shuddered. 'Guess I thought I was booked for the devil's home all right when I woke up and found myself in that awful cave alone with him!'

Miss Nalder looked interested, but Frieda, at a touch from Jo, changed the conversation by pointing out a white road, winding up the mountain-side. 'That is the way we go,' she said; 'up there as far as you can see. Then, when we pass a bend in the road that carries it right to the other slopes, we pass a tiny village where one of the greatest wood-carvers in Tirol was born—Gottlieb Strönen. In the church, there is a tablet carved in Spanish walnut and set in the north wall, saying that he was baptised in that church, and, later, buried in the graveyard.'

'I've read somewhere,' said Joey, 'that he carved a pot of roses so marvellously that the flowers trembled in a high wind.'

'That is something like what has been said of Grinling

Gibbons, the great English architect,' said Miss Nalder. 'Have any of you read *The Carved Cartoon*?'

For a wonder, not even Jo had seen it, and she was an omnivorous reader. Miss Nalder was surprised. 'What? None of you? Oh, this will never do!' she declared. 'I am surprised at *you*, Joey! I was sure *you* would know it. It's a delightful story—based on Grinling Gibbon's life. It gives a vivid picture of the Great Plague and of the Fire of London. I must send home for my copy, and lend it to you. I know you'll like it.'

'Is it historical, then?' asked Jo eagerly. 'How topping! Yes, *do* send for it, Miss Nalder—*please*! I'd just love to read it!'

'I should like it too,' said Frieda; and Elsie, and one or two of the rest said the same.

'I'll wait and see if it's lessony,' said lazy Evadne cautiously.

'Not a bit,' Miss Nalder assured her. 'Very well, Jo. As soon as we have camped and finished our arrangements, I'll write a post-card, and ask them to send it at once.'

'Oh, thank you, Miss Nalder!' Jo, who was 'history-mad,' as the rest were wont to declare, slipped into a happy dream. She loved reading of all kind, but especially on historical subjects. More! she was projecting a story with a historical background, and had, even now, two chapters of it written. She sat in rapture from which she did not awaken till a cry from Frieda of 'Here we are! This is as far as the charabancs can go! We must walk the rest of the way!' aroused her to the fact that they were standing still on the broad white road, with a pine-wood to the right, and a steep mountain-side, rocky and bare, to the left, while, in the distance, she could see peaks rising above peaks, with, here and there, the silvery gleam that told of eternal snows or great glaciers lying in the intense silence that prevails at such heights.

Jo followed the others out of the charabanc to the road, and then helped to pile up the knapsacks on the roadside. There was no time for more dreaming. They all thronged about, laughing and chattering as they shouldered their burdens. Then they formed, two and two, and filed along the narrow woodland-path through the black trees, where, once more, the aromatic perfume of the pines filled the air, and fallen pine-needles rustled underfoot. It was a pleasant walk, and they were glad to stretch their legs after the three hours of sitting still.

They were well on their way, when Joey suddenly stood still, with a cry.

'What on earth's the matter?' demanded Grizel, who was close behind and had nearly fallen over her. 'Bitten by something?'

'That village—the village where Gottlieb Strönen was born and buried!' cried Jo. 'I missed it! Oh—and I did so want to see it!'

'Where were your eyes?' asked Miss Wilson crisply. 'I suppose you were in a dream as usual.'

Pretty Miss Stewart smiled sympathetically. 'Hard lines, Joey! Never mind; we are sure to make an expedition to it one day, so you'll see it then.'

'You were thinking, my Jo?' asked Simone Lecoutier, a slim French girl, who had a deep adoration for Jo that had grown with their five years together. 'What was it, then?'

'Something Nally said—a book she's going to send for and lend us,' said Jo. 'Come on Simone! We can't hang about. Besides, I'm jolly hungry, now I come to think of it, and I want *Mittagessen*, I can tell you.'

Her words reminded all who heard them that they were hungry too, and they pressed on as rapidly as the captain and the two lieutenants would permit. It seemed as if they would never leave the trees. Then, suddenly, the forest vanished. They were on the borders of a little grassy meadow, and before them, shining silver in the glow of the warm August sun, was the Baumersee, still, beautiful, and gleaming.

CHAPTER V

CAMPING

WITH a cry of delight, the girls ran across the meadow to the margin of the lake, noting its beauties with eyes trained to see the lovelinesses of nature.

Packs were dropped, and they stood for a moment in silence, which was eventually broken by Cornelia. 'Say! I guess this is a knock-out!' she remarked cheerfully. 'I guess the Saints will be mad *they* couldn't come with us when we tell them next term.'

Evadne joined her. 'It isn't a mite lovelier than our own lake, but I like it for a change. Guess we're going to have a bully time here.'

Frieda, Simone, Joey, and Marie von Eschenau moved a little apart from the noisy middles.

'It's beautiful,' said Jo softly. 'I know you said it was wonderful, Frieda; but you never said it was *so* wonderful.'

'It is almost perfect,' added Marie. 'So still and peaceful—so—so——'

'So—*calm*,' said Simone.

That, indeed, was the atmosphere of the little lake. Ringed round by the great limestone mountains, neither village nor hamlet in sight, and no lake-steamers to break up the smooth sheen of its mirror-like surface into ripples, it seemed to lie far away from the world and all troubling things. It was not well known, and very few tourists ever found their way to its quiet shores. The girls were to find that they had it almost wholly to themselves. Two or three farms lay beyond it, over a spur of the mountain whose steep slope was washed by its waters on the side opposite the pine-wood; but the inhabitants were usually too busy to trouble with it. The nearest village was a league away; and it was a small one, consisting only of twenty houses, a church, and a little building

35

where the children went to school in the winter. There was not even a priest there, the village sharing the ministrations of the priest from Mühlstaub, a somewhat larger place, five miles farther north.

For a few minutes Guides and Guiders gazed intently at the loveliness round them. Then Miss Wilson, bethinking herself that the day was already well advanced, called to the girls to come and prepare for a meal. 'You will have plenty of opportunities for looking at it, and it is a long time since your last solid meal,' she said sensibly. 'Come along, girls!'

They came—albeit unwillingly—for 'Bill' was not to be gainsaid. She soon had them all back in the meadow and hard at work. Jo and Frieda were set to building a camp fireplace with some stones which the nearest farmer had caused to be brought there earlier in the day, while Simone, with a specially picked party of juniors, went to the woods for sticks. Juliet Carrick and Grizel Cochrane unpacked hampers and baskets; and Carla von Flügen and Eva von Heiling set to work to spread out the lengths of American-cloth which were to serve as tablecloths, and lay the ground-sheets at either side of them for the girls to sit on. Sundry of the younger Guides placed mugs and plates down the American-cloths, and others were busy filling the big dixie with water from a nearby spring, and laying out the sandwiches and fruit which had been brought for their first meal.

'Thank goodness, we shan't have far to go for water,' said Jo presently, pushing her hair back from her hot face, and adding a smudge to its beauties as she did so. 'Now then, you people, where are those sticks? Hurry up with them, or there'll be no coffee for anyone.'

Simone came racing up with an armful of twigs, followed by Margia Stevens; then came Berta Hamel and Hilda Bhaer, two quiet people, who never gave any trouble, and Ilonka Barkocz, a Hungarian girl, who was good enough when she was not with the set ruled by Margia Stevens.

'Here are the sticks!' panted Simone. 'Cyrilla and Violet are bringing some big branches along to put on when the fire is really burning.'

36

'Thank you, Simone,' said Frieda. "Will you not stay and help us build it? There is enough here for a while.'

'But not nearly enough to last the afternoon,' added Miss Stewart, as she came across to them, carrying a large can of milk. 'You will need a great deal more than that, girls.'

Simone sighed. 'I wish wood did not burn away so quickly. Shall we go and get some more, Madame?'

'No; I think that Frieda is right, and it will do for the present,' said Miss Stewart, with an amused glance at the French girl. She knew, like most of the others, that Simone was wildly jealous of Jo's other friendships. There had been 'scenes' in the past over the head-girl's firm determination to have as many and what friends she liked. Those were over, for Simone had learned self-control during her years at school. But she had a positive genius for making herself miserable if she thought Jo was too much with anyone else, and Miss Stewart, though she was rather scornful about this, was too kind-hearted to want to spoil the French child's fortnight. So she said no more about further fuel-gathering, and Simone settled down happily to helping Jo and Frieda make the fire burn.

It was soon blazing away with a heat that was uncomfortable, though the stillness of the day prevented much smoke. The resinous wood brought from the pine-woods was dry, and burned easily. Before long they were able to set the two dixies—one of water and the other of milk—on the stones, and then, while some of the juniors fed the blaze, the elder girls went to help cut bread and butter and cake, and fill the tin bowls with the small sugar-slabs which, on the Continent, take the place of our sparkling lumps. The milk and water soon boiled, and then Miss Wilson, who had been preparing the coffee, came to the rescue, and, with the help of Grizel, lifted the milk dixie off the fire and poured the milk on her mixture. Water was added, and then the whole was poured back and set to boil up again. After this it was pronounced ready, and the girls hastened to gather round the American-cloth strips. All stood with bent heads and folded hands while the captain spoke the short Latin grace without which they never had a meal. That over, they dropped down on the ground-sheets, while Grizel and Juliet filled the mugs and passed them along, and when all were served they started on their meal.

'Isn't this jolly?' said Anne Seymour, who was sitting back to back with her great friend, Louise Redfield.

'Topping,' agreed Louise. 'Ow! Don't wriggle, Anne. You nearly had my coffee over.'

'Well, you're digging your elbows into me,' protested Louise. '*That's* better!' as, disregarding all Anne's protests, she twisted herself into a more comfortable position.

'I didn't know I was so thirsty,' said Jo, after she had drained her mug. 'Any more coffee, Juliet?'

'Plenty; but you'll have to get up and help yourself,' said Juliet. 'I'm much too comfy to move.'

'Lazy object!' laughed Jo, as she got to her feet. 'Being engaged is not improving you, my child. It will be my painful duty to write to Donal and lecture him on spoiling you—and I can see that!'

'Joey—if you dare!' cried Juliet, who, being very newly engaged, and also well aware that with Joey to think was to act, was completely upset by this speech.

'Then show yourself a decent sport,' retorted Joey. 'A Guide's duty is to help others!'

'Then help Juliet by waiting on yourself, lazybones,' said Grizel, coming to Juliet's assistance. 'You surely didn't come to camp to be run after?'

Jo filled her mug and set down the big enamelled jug, in which the coffee had been put, before replying. Then she fixed Grizel with her eyes, and grinned as she said, 'Example is better than precept, my child. Likewise, practise what you preach. It's up to you!'

She got no satisfaction, however. Grizel merely hunched herself into a more comfortable position before she murmured, 'It's too hot to argue. Go and sit down, child, before you spill that coffee.'

Jo flushed up, but went back to her seat on the ground-sheet without replying. Simone, indignant at Grizel's cavalier treatment, was prepared to rush to her defence, but Frieda the peaceful restrained her. 'Don't Simone! It would do no good, and only annoy Grizel. Jo does not really mind, and she and Grizel have never been very friendly.'

Simone forbore, though her eyes sparkled angrily, and, as Jo sat down with them with great nonchalance and began to chatter about something else at once, the affair passed over. But the Guiders had noticed it, and discussed it later.

'Grizel had no right to call Jo "child," like that,' declared Miss Stewart.

'Apart from anything else, Jo is head-girl, and it isn't good for some of those young monkeys of middles to hear her addressed like that. Aren't you going to speak to her, Bill?'

Miss Wilson frowned. 'It's difficult. Grizel will be on the Staff next term, and she's not a child now. She would resent being spoken to. I don't quite know what to do.'

'Not if you spoke as commandant,' urged 'Charlie,' with whom Jo was a great favourite, while she was not fond of Grizel. 'I really think you ought to, Bill.'

'What do you think, Nally?' asked Miss Wilson.

Miss Nalder was decided. 'I agree with Charlie. Anyway, it isn't next term yet. Grizel isn't on the Staff till then. Besides, she and Juliet Carrick won't be at the school, but at the annexe, and that's a very different matter.'

'I don't like to begin by scolding, though,' said Miss Wilson. 'No, you two; I think I'll overlook it this time. But if it occurs again, I shall certainly speak to Grizel.'

'Well, you know best; and you're commandant too,' said Miss Stewart. 'But tell me, was Grizel Cochrane always like this when she was at school? I wasn't here then, you know, and I'm beginning to think I've missed a somewhat unpleasant time.'

'Oh, Grizel has always been a bit of a firebrand,' replied Miss Wilson. 'I shall never forget my first term at the Chalet School! Oh, nothing really bad happened so far as Grizel was concerned; but she was a prefect, and head of the games, and it went to her head, I think. She really was unbearably conceited that term!'

'That was the term before she was head-girl, wasn't it?'

asked Miss Nalder. 'I seem to have heard some wild story of how Grizel nearly missed it.'

'Oh, we never talk of that,' said Miss Wilson quickly. 'Madame and Mademoiselle decided to forget, so we all did. I doubt if most of the School ever heard of it.'

'I certainly never did till this moment,' said 'Charlie.' 'All right, Bill; we won't go on with the subject. Instead, let's go and rouse those children and see about getting the tents pitched, shall we?'

'It would be best,' agreed 'Bill,' as she got to her feet and stretched. 'It's far too hot for any of us to remain in full uniform. The sooner we all change into overalls, the better. And we can't do that until we've somewhere to change. Do you know if the men have brought everything yet?'

'They came just before we sent the girls to rest,' said Miss Nalder. 'They brought Rufus, too, so Jo's cup of joy was full. She took him off with her, and she and her crush are over there in the shade somewhere.' She waved her hand vaguely in the direction of the pine-wood as she spoke.

'I know,' said the captain. 'I begged Madame to let us have him. A dog is always a protection, and Rufus particularly so. Jo knew he was coming—at least, I expect she did.'

'If her joy on seeing him is anything by which to judge, she didn't,' said Miss Nalder, as she set off towards the heap of tents, tent-poles, and other paraphernalia.

Miss Wilson laughed, and then blew her whistle. A moment later the quiet meadow was covered with girls racing towards her from all corners. 'Come along, girls,' she said, when they were all within earshot. 'We've got to get these tents up, and you've had a good rest now. Let me see; there are four tents to hold six each. Two to hold three; two for two; and my own. Then there's the big tent for the commissariat, and the spare one for sitting in if it rains. They must all be up to-night, as well as all the rest of the camp buildings. Which of you people have learned how to pitch a tent?'

All the elder girls knew, and most of the younger ones had helped during the little week-end camps they had had during the previous term. They divided themselves into parties, and soon were busily at work, digging holes for the centre-poles. The two big tents for the commissariat and recreation tents had ridge-poles, and the captain judged it best to attend to them herself, with the other two Guiders, Juliet and Grizel, to help. She set Greta, Violet, Ruth, and the Dutch child, Lilli van Huysen, to sorting out the pegs, since these girls were the youngest in the camp, and she had no wish for them to overtire themselves. Elisaveta and Jo were requested to see to the fire, which by this time had sunk to a glowing mass and needed feeding. The rest were employed in opening out the canvas, while the strongest set the poles, and great was the confusion with ropes before even one tent was on its pole. Once it was, however, the pegs were soon in and the guy-ropes fixed. Before long, the little encampment began to look quite businesslike, and when Jo, disgusted at being relegated to the duty of fire-warden, came to ask for a more useful job, the eleven tents were erected, and Miss Nalder was going round them with a mallet, driving the pegs in as far as she could.

'Can't I help?' asked Jo. 'The fire's all right now, and we've got the dixie on for *Kaffee.*'

'You can carry these trestles into the commissariat-tent, and help to put the planks on them if you like,' said Miss Wilson. 'I want the food off the ground as soon as possible.'

Jo set off joyfully, and for an hour and a half the little valley buzzed with excitement and chatter as the girls worked to get their camp into ship-shape condition. It was done at last, and very nice everything looked. The tents had been pitched with flaps opening to the east, since, in that way, they faced the forest, and so would gain some protection if rain were to come. The commissariat-tent was at the back; then the recreation-tent; in front of them came the sleeping-tents. Nearer the lake were the two flag-poles, and the flags would be run up at six o'clock the next morning. Between them, the commandant would take her stand when she took Prayers, and there was a little prominence in the ground at this point which, as Juliet said, might have been intended for such a thing. The camp-fire was a little away from the tents; and, some fifty or a hundred yards from it, was the incinerator in which they would burn all the rubbish.

'It looks something like a camp!' said Joey proudly, as she finally came out of the commissariat-tent, her sleeves rolled up to her shoulders, her hair standing up on end, and a streak of *something* across her nose. 'Isn't it hot working, though?—Madame,' she turned to Miss Wilson, 'it's been gorgeous to-day. Can't we bathe? I feel too sticky and greasy to *live*!'

For answer, Miss Wilson looked at Frieda. 'How is the lake fed, Frieda? Do you know?'

'By a stream that flows into it from that end, Madame,' replied Frieda. 'There are no springs here, as with our own lake. I have bathed in it before in the summer, and it was almost warm.'

'Very well, then,' said the captain, with a nod. 'We'll sponge off the worst of the dirt from our hands and faces, and have *Kaffee*. Then, after we've washed up and left everything tidy, we'll run down and try the water.'

A cheer greeted her words, and the girls made for the camp-fire, where the two dixies were again boiling—this time only with water. They emptied one, and Miss Nalder filled it up with the milky coffee to heat for their afternoon meal, while they washed in the hot water, and then tidied their hair and generally made themselves neat. By the time they were ready, the coffee was ready too, and two or three who had not had so much to do as the others, or had got the hot water first, put out the baskets with their twists of fancy bread, and set the mugs in shining rows on the grass.

'Washing up first, girls,' cried Miss Wilson, when they had finished and were piling the things together. 'Then a short rest, and after that a bathe. It's half-past four now, so that means we go in at half-past five. Only a short bathe to-day, as we're so late, so I shall call you all out when you have been in a quarter of an hour. We must be dressed for the Angelus at six—eighteen, if you prefer our own time,' she added, with a smile at Jo, whose face expressed disgust at the use of English time.

42

'I like things to be the same in their own countries,' said that young lady in an anything but lucid aside to Simone.

'In other words, "When in Rome, do as the Romans do," ' laughed 'Charlie,' who had overheard her. 'Quite right, Jo.—Now then, you people, hurry up, or we shall be late.'

With this, she swept them away, and they hurried off to help with the washing up, while the Guiders drew together to discuss the question of 'fatigues.' They soon had this matter settled, and were considering the question of church-parade, when Miss Nalder suddenly cried out, 'What are we to do about Prayers?'

'Do about Prayers? My dear girl what do you mean?' demanded Miss Wilson.

'Well, Charlie's a Catholic; *you're* a Catholic; *I'm* a Catholic. There isn't one Protestant Guider among us. What happens to the Protestant girls?'

Miss Wilson looked troubled. 'I hadn't thought of that.'

'Neither had I.' Miss Stewart knitted her brows. 'How are we to manage? Of course, if it were only girls like Jo Bettany it wouldn't matter. She attends Mass almost as often as her own service. But there are Violet Allison and Ruth Wynyard, and Lilli van Huysen——'

'And Evadne and Cornelia,' added Miss Nalder. 'Elsie Carr would join with us, I know. Didn't she go with you at Oberammergau, and again when you were at Fulpmes?'

'Yes. But those other five are a different matter. What can we do?'

They thought a moment. Then Miss Wilson's face suddenly cleared. 'I don't know what we are making all this fuss about. Both Grizel and Juliet are Protestants, and they must take service for their own people between them.'

'Good idea!' exclaimed Miss Stewart. 'It will do them good, too.'

'Well, we've settled *that*. Is there anything else we ought to decide? No? Then let's get our young mermaids into the water. They are all longing to be there, I know.'

And the Guiders, with the last organising difficulty settled, ran off to call the girls and send them to their tents to change into bathing-suits before they all took to the water like so many fishes.

CHAPTER VI

THE FIRST NIGHT IN CAMP

IT was glorious in the water. Unlike the spring-fed Tiernsee, the Baumersee is a warm lake, and the girls frolicked about in the water joyously. The captain would only permit the fifteen minutes' bathing, it is true. As she said, they had had the three hours' journey, and then all the hard work of pitching camp, and it would not do for them to overtire themselves by much swimming and diving. But she promised that they should bathe again on the morrow, and they came out when the whistle blew, and fled back to their tents to dry and dress, fresh and glowing.

'I suppose it's just as well to go slowly,' said Joey Bettany, as she fastened up her overall. 'We don't want to go home a company of wrecks, or our people will lay the law down about camping.'

'There is the whistle for the Angelus,' said Frieda, hurriedly tying the ends of her plaits. 'I am ready now, Simone. Will you come?—Are you coming, Jo?'

'Of course!' And Joey stuck in her Guide badge and ran out after them. Most of the girls were there, and the short prayer was soon over. When it was finished, the girls scattered, some to get sticks, others to bring water, others to find the way to the farm whence they were to have butter and milk and eggs.

'Mind you don't lose yourselves,' was Miss Wilson's last remark, as Juliet went off with Jo, Elisaveta, Evadne, and Elsie. 'You can bring as much milk as you can carry —it won't be wasted! Sure you have sufficient money?'

'Heaps!' said Juliet gaily. 'What about eggs, Madame?'

'Bill' looked at the quartette and smiled. 'I think not. You and Jo will have to carry the milk, and I shouldn't like to think of Evadne and Elsie carrying a few dozen eggs between them. We don't want omelettes on the way back to camp!'

'That's mean,' said Evadne under her breath to Elsie. 'Guess we could carry eggs as well as anyone else.'

'Well, there'll be the butter to bring, anyhow,' said Elsie pacifically. 'Seven kilos of butter——'

'*What?*' demanded Jo, overhearing this last. 'D'you think we're young lorries to carry all that?'

'I don't know. That's what Bill said, anyhow!' retorted Elsie.

'She said no such thing,' replied the headgirl. 'We don't have to bring seven litres of milk *or* seven kilos of butter. It's just as well you two aren't going on your own, I think.'

'Well, we've got to carry whatever it is we've to get,' argued the Princess suddenly. 'O-o-oh, Joey Here's Rufus coming!'

And there, sure enough, was Rufus. He had enjoyed a swim with his mistress, and had soon shaken his thick, heavy coat dry. Now, he had no idea of missing the chance of a walk with her. During term-time he was kept up at the Sonnalpe, and saw too little of her as it was. Here, he meant to spend every moment possible with her. So he came bounding along, a magnificent specimen of his breed, with a great head, huge bone, and the deep bay of his tribe. He was quite a young dog— only four years old—and he adored Jo, who had saved him from drowning when he was a four-week-old puppy, as related in another chronicle of the Chalet School.

Jo shook her fist at him. 'You villain!' she said. 'And I thought you were safely asleep in the tent. Oh well, it's too hot to trail back with you, so you'll just have to come. Thank goodness you can behave yourself, anyhow, and don't chase chickens or sheep!'

From her tone, Rufus judged that he was forgiven, so he pressed close to her side, wagging his great tail and regarding the world with an amiable if somewhat foolish smile.

'That dog just worships you, Jo,' observed Juliet.

'Of course he does! Don't I adore him?' demanded

45

Joey. 'He's the best tyke in all this world, and he knows it.—Don't you, old man?'

Rufus 'wuffed' joyfully, and they went on. They reached the farm safely, and got their butter and milk from a voluble farmer's wife, who exclaimed at their dress, at the size of Rufus, and at their daring in camping out thus. She took them into the kitchen, and made them sit down and drink big mugs of sweet rich milk, warm from the cow. Even Rufus was given a bowlful, much to his joy.

'For well-wishing and good luck,' she remarked, as he lapped it up. 'But, *mein Fräulein,* what if the rain comes?'

'Sit in our tents,' said Joey, finishing the last of her milk with an effort, for the mugs were generous ones, and had been brimful. 'We shall be quite safe and dry there, *meine Frau.*'

The good woman shook her head. It was more than she could understand. However, these were undoubtedly foreigners, and one had heard of the mad ways of foreigners before this. Of her own accord, she offered to send over six dozen eggs the next morning, when her man would be going that way on an errand. Juliet closed with the offer at once, and then they left.

'Well, I hope she's not going to give us milk in such quantities always,' remarked Elsie, as they walked back through the pine-woods. 'I feel as if I might burst at any moment.'

'I feel rather that way myself,' acknowledged Juliet. 'But it was nice milk—thick with cream.'

'And yellow,' supplemented Jo. 'It was almost primrose colour.'

'*I* think it's a good thing the milk-pails have lids,' observed the Princess, who was stalking along with a basket containing a big slab of butter, while Juliet, Jo, and Elsie carried the two milk-pails between them, and Evadne brought up the rear with more butter. 'You three are swinging them like fun. It'll be butter, not milk, by the time we get back to camp—unless you're careful, that is.'

The three stopped swinging the pails, and went on more carefully. It was sunset by the time they got back, and the wonderful colours of the sky were reflected in the lake. A huge pile of twigs and sticks was at one side of the fireplace, and another lay near the incinerator. Even as the five came into camp, there was a yell, and Cornelia, Violet, Ruth, and the usually quiet Hilda Bhaer came tearing back from another part of the forest, laden with more fuel.

'I say, are we going to have a bonfire?' demanded Elsie.

'No; but singsong after *Abendessen*,' said Violet, shaken out of her usual shyness by the jolly atmosphere of the camp. 'Madame said we might for first night.'

'Juliet—Ju-li-et!' It was Grizel's voice that came floating to them from the commissariat-tent.

'Well, what is it?' shouted back Juliet.

'Do you know where the cocoa is? I can't find it anywhere.'

'Jo, you put the things away.' Juliet turned to Jo. 'Where is the cocoa?'

'Cocoa?' Jo looked dense.

'Yes—cocoa. C-o-c-o-a, cocoa! Got it *now*?'

'Far as I know, I never saw any.'

'*What?*'

'I never saw any. Gone suddenly deaf?'

'But it *must* be there! Charlie ought to know, for she ordered a huge tin of it. She told me to mix it now for *Abendessen*,' cried Grizel.

Jo collapsed on the short, thyme-bedecked turf, and began to laugh. Juliet shook her indignantly. 'Get up, Jo, and stop that idiotic gurgling! Where is it? Has anyone been playing pranks?'

Jo wriggled to her feet, and faced her friend. '*I* haven't, if that's what you mean. I don't know where it is—sitting at home, I should imagine. I know I never put it away, for it wasn't there to put.'

Juliet and Grizel faced each other, consternation in their faces. 'No cocoa! What on earth are we to do?' gasped the former.

'Go and tell Charlie, I should think.' Jo put her oar in.

'Who was supposed to pack it?' asked Grizel.

'I haven't the slightest idea,' observed Juliet. 'I did the

47

tinned fruits, and all the dry stuff like flour and sugar and——'

'Then it was *your* job.'

Juliet looked downcast. Grizel began to rummage along the trestle-and-board shelves again. Jo started fresh chuckles, observing, 'This is what comes of being engaged! I suppose you were so busy thinking of Donal that you didn't bother whether everying was there or not.'

Juliet turned on her coldly. 'That is not funny, Jo. It is even verging on the vulgar. If you *must* be funny, at least try to avoid vulgarity, *please*!'

Jo flushed. But she knew how her sister regarded such talk, so she swallowed her wrath, and said nothing. Fortunately, Miss Stewart, wondering why they were so long in getting the cocoa, came along to see what was happening, and saved further squabbling. 'What *are* you doing, girls? Everyone is ready, and the milk is boiling as hard as it can go. Where is the cocoa? Fetch it along, and hurry up about it.'

Juliet gulped. 'It's not there, Madame.'

'Not there?' Miss Stewart stared. 'But I ordered it when I ordered all the other things. Surely they didn't forget to send it?'

'They didn't,' said Jo. 'I saw it on the kitchen table at "Die Rosen" when I went to see the stores. But we've forgotten to pack it. It's where it was—unless Marie has moved it,' she added.

Miss Stewart looked at them helplessly. 'How could you forget it? And what are we to do for to-night? I can get some more in the morning from the village. But what about to-night?'

'We must drink hot milk, I suppose,' said Jo gloomily. 'Goodness knows I had enough for one meal at the farm. Still, it won't kill us for once.'

'I'm so sorry, Miss Stewart,' said Juliet. 'It is my fault, of course. You trusted me to see to the packing of the dry things, and I must have forgotten it somehow.'

'Well, it's not much use worrying about it now,' said Miss Stewart. 'We must do as Jo says—drink hot milk to-night, and get some from the village in the morning. —Jo, you can write home, and ask them to bring it when they come on Saturday. We can manage till then.'

'Then, as we haven't to bother with making cocoa, we'd better go and see about getting the milk poured out,' said Grizel, leaving the tent as she spoke.

Jo followed her, and Juliet was left alone with Miss Stewart. 'I'm so sorry, Madame. I can't think how I came to be such an idiot. It's not even as if it were a small tin that you could overlook—it isn't!'

'Never mind,' said Miss Stewart. 'We can't expect everything to go like clockwork all the time. Come along, Juliet, and don't pull such a long face. The girls must learn to take vicissitudes as well as joys. Come—"A Guide laughs and sings on all occasions," you know. And it might have been worse. It might have been something really important—like the hams, for instance, or the jam.'

Thus adjured, Juliet relaxed her brows, smiled, and followed the Guider to where the Guides were all sitting, holding out their mugs, while Grizel passed up and down the ranks with a big jug, filling them. Joey and Frieda were helping her, and despite the lack of the cocoa, no one looked upset.

Supper went with a swing, and when it was over and they had washed up and put everything ready for the night, they gathered round the camp-fire in a double circle and Miss Wilson started them on a round. 'Come along girls! "Camp-fire's burning!" You all know the words?'

They all did, and she separated them into three groups, and soon had them singing gaily. They followed it up with the old English madrigal, 'Sumer is Icumen in,' and after that, 'The Hart he Loves the High Wood.' This over, there were loud calls for Joey, who was the recognised soloist on these occasions.

'Come along, Jo!' said Miss Stewart. 'Do you want an accompaniment?'

'For "Ye Banks and Braes"—yes, please,' said Jo.

The girls were accustomed to this. Dividing into four parts, they hummed softly the running accompaniment, while Jo's golden voice rang out in the old song. They were well trained at school, their singing-master being a
49

musician to his finger-tips, with a wonderful knowledge of the possibilities of the human voice, and the gift of teaching. Such music had rarely been heard at the Baumersee, and it carried far on the still night-air. By twos and threes the people from the farms crept up through the woods, and peeped between the trees at the sight so strange to them. The warm, red glow of the fire lit up the camp, casting lights and shadows across the young faces, bringing out the lights in Marie's golden curls and Frieda's flaxen plaits; touching the glory of Giovanna Donati's Titian locks; giving warmth and colour to the scene. Curled up at one side of the fire, her head a little back, was Jo, the music pouring from her parted lips, while her black eyes were soft with dreams. Beside her crouched the Princess, her forgotten milk at her feet, one hand on Jo's lap, her deep brown eyes fixed on the absorbed face of the singer. Frieda and Marie with their marked fairness gave balance to the group. At the other side sat Guiders—big Miss Stewart, with her boyish prettiness; quiet Miss Wilson; little Miss Nalder, as rosy and trim as a pink-tipped daisy. Between were the mass of the girls, all listening intently to Jo's song, as she sang alone and unaccompanied Schubert's surpassingly lovely 'Hark, Hark, the Lark!'

'Now it's someone else's turn!' she cried, as the last notes died in the night. 'Come along, Corney! Pipe up!'

No one was ever shy at singsong, so Cornelia obliged with 'Clementine,' in which the whole camp roared the chorus.

One or two of the others sang also, but Jo, as Grizel remarked, was the prima-donna of the occasion. Her voice held some of the ethereal purity of a choir-boy's, and song seemed to bubble from her lips as readily as speech. They sang till Miss Wilson suddenly recalled the fact that they had all had an early start and a long day. She jumped to her feet, despite the chorus of protests that arose, and summoned them hastily to ranks for Prayers. The unbidden audience, realising that the concert was over for the night, stole away, and it was not till some days later that the girls knew that it had been there. Meanwhile, the big storm-lanterns had been lighted in the tents and the girls were undressing rapidly.

'I don't believe I'll ever stay on that thing,' said Elsie Carr, as she surveyed her somewhat corpulent palliasse with its stuffing of straw.

'I told you you'd put far too much in,' said Margia, who was now in her pyjamas and preparing to say her prayers. 'You'd better take some of it out.'

With a deep sigh Elsie finished her undressing, and then began to do as she was told. She was still at it when 'Lights out' rang out, and the others had to come hastily to the rescue. After something like a scrimmage they got the thing right, and Elsie lay down and began to fold her blankets over her. When Miss Wilson came to the tent it was in darkness, and the girls were all tucked up more or less comfortably. She flashed her electric torch over each one, and made sure that they were comparatively safe from rolling out during the night. Then she wished them 'Good-night!' and withdrew to the next tent. Five minutes later, as the girls were still murmuring to themselves and giggling. 'Taps' sounded, sung by the three Guiders, Juliet, Grizel, and the four cadets. Joey's lovely voice led them, and the rest sounded somehow unearthly to the girls in the tents, coming through the firelit darkness of the August night. The tent-flaps were up, and they could see 'a wonderful clear night of stars' outside. Very clearly the words came over to them, mingling with the night-sounds, and becoming part of them.

'Good-night, everybody,' said Evadne, when it was over.

"Good-night,' chorused the others. And they soon fell asleep, for they were tired out with the day's activities.

Meantime, in one of the tents for three, Joey, Frieda, and Simone were slipping between their blankets, while Marie von Eschenau was tucking herself up in the one she shared with Anne Seymour and Louise Redfield. Grizel and Juliet had one of the double tents and Miss Nalder and Miss Stewart shared the other, Miss Wilson, as commandant, having her own little private tent to herself.

Rufus, who had been set loose, laid himself across the opening of the tent in which his mistress was, gave a deep sigh as he stretched himself on his side, and fell into the light sleep of a watchful dog. There was silence everywhere, broken only by the soft lapping of the water and an occasional 'hush-hush' of the breeze through the grass and flowers in the meadow.

The whole camp must have been slumbering soundly for at least three hours, when Rufus suddenly stirred and growled softly, his head raised, his nostrils snuffing an alien scent. No one moved, for all were too deeply asleep. Rufus slowly got to his feet, and padded noiselessly over to the commissariat-tent, whence the scent came. It seemed to vanish, and he was about to turn and go back to his place, when he got it full in the face, and promptly began barking with a vim that roused the echoes, and brought everyone in camp to her senses. Elsie rolled out from her blankets and made for the door, still trailing one of them after her. Jo leapt to her feet, crashed into the pole, and nearly brought the tent down on top of them all. Cries and exclamations came from the others; and the Staff hastened out to where the big dog was standing, baying furiously.

'Someone in the commissariat-tent!' cried Miss Stewart, who had hastily pulled on a raincoat over her pyjamas.

'Girls! Go back to your tents and stay there!" ordered Miss Wilson, who had seized a Guide stave and was making for the commissariat-tent. 'Jo, call Rufus off! We don't want any tragedies.'

Jo rushed out, caught her dog round the neck, and held him firmly. 'He'll be all right now. I can hold him, though I can't drag him away.'

The three Guiders went cautiously to the tent, and 'Bill,' deepening her voice till was almost baritone, called, 'Who is there?—*Wer ist es?*'

There was no answer, and Jo was having her work cut out to hold Rufus, who was becoming more and more excited, with his hackles up on end and his eyes glowing red. 'Miss Wilson,' she cried, 'I don't believe it's a human at all! Rufus is behaving as though it were another dog. I can feel him—simply dying to fight—Frieda! For goodness' sake come and help me hold him!'

Frieda, Marie, and Simone all flung themselves on Rufus, and the four girls held him firmly, while Miss Wilson and Miss Stewart, backed up by Miss Nalder, Juliet, and Grizel, all of them carrying staves, stalked up to the tent and undid the fastenings. Just then there was a terrified yelp, and a small dog whom Jo had noticed at the farm while they were getting the butter and milk, dashed madly forth from under one of the walls, and shot across the meadow as if wolves were at his heels.

At sight of his foe escaping him thus, Rufus forgot his manners, and with a wrathful '*Woof!*' hurtled after him, dragging the four girls who had attached themselves to his shaggy coat and were so taken by surprise that they could not help themselves. They let go in a second, however, and collapsed in a wildly giggling heap on each other, while Rufus, freed at last, crossed the meadow at his best pace, woofing indignantly at intervals.

"Call him back, Joey! cried Grizel. 'He'll slay that infant!'

Joey made no reply, which was not wonderful, considering that she had the toes of Frieda's right foot across her mouth and her nose rubbed into the ground, while Simone was gripping her hair under the impression that it was Rufus's coat.

When at length she contrived to get to her feet, the chase was over, and Rufus was coming back, a crestfallen and shamefaced dog. The small white mongrel, inspired with panic, and with much less weight to carry, had fled like a streak of lightning through the forest, and finished up by diving into a stream and swimming frantically away from that terrible place that was so full of nice smells and horrible noises. Rufus, suddenly coming to his senses, realised that he had forgotten to be a gentleman, and sneaked back to receive his scolding.

He never got it, however, for the Guiders were so thankful to learn that he was such an excellent watch that he was patted and told he was 'a good old fellow!' Jo hugged him vehemently, and his chief friends among the girls fussed over him till he felt rather bored; and gently freeing himself from their attentions, he trotted back to his post at the door of the tent. The captain was recalled to the hour of night by Rufus's behaviour, and promptly sent the girls back to their tents, with instructions to go to sleep at once and not utter a word. They went, and, in spite of the fact that most of them thought it would be impossible to sleep after all that excitement, it is on record that the majority of them had to be *shaken* awake the next morning. The reveillé didn't reach them at all.

CHAPTER VII

JOEY HAS AN ADVENTURE

BY the end of the second day the Chalet School Guides had settled down, and felt as though they had been camping most of their lives. Inspection had been rather a trying affair, for the time allotted to the tidying up of the tents had been all too short for some of the more untidy members. The captain had had one or two rather scathing remarks to make about unbrushed shoes, bedding not folded properly, and tents not in that meticulous order which she warned them she would expect for the future. But when it was over the girls were allowed to scatter on their various fatigues without feeling unduly depressed over their shortcomings.

The duties of bringing milk and butter from the farm were deputed to Grizel Cochrane and four junior Guides. Marie von Eschenau, Anne Seymour, Elsie Carr, Paula von Rothenfels, Margia Stevens, and the Princess were the cooks for the day; Joey Bettany headed the wood-gathering party, which numbered ten people. The resinous twigs and branches they brought burned quickly, and there was the fire in the incinerator to consider, as well as the camp-fire. Miss Wilson decided that they must have two huge cairns of wood which would suffice for the day. Water was brought from the spring by Eva von Heiling, Frieda Mensch, and Ilonka Barkocz. Washing-up was given over bodily to the Rose Patrol, under the leadership of Bianca di Ferrara, a gentle Italian girl, who was always thankful that her patrol contained none of the fire-brands, such as Margia Stevens, Elsie Carr, or the two young Americans. These four led most of the other middles by the nose as a general rule, and could be relied on to think of mischievous pranks which no one else had ever imagined, and which, accordingly, had not been forbidden. Bianca, surveying her five lambs —the other three had not come to camp—heaved a sigh of relief and set to work to wash plates and mugs and cutlery, while the rest dried and put them away.

Mittagessen that day would consist of cold lamb which had been cooked at home, boiled potatoes, and wild strawberries, which grew in abundance in a field not far from where they were. All those not detailed for any special duty were given baskets and cans and sent to this field, with instructions that they were not to return till the various receptacles were filled. The milk-and-butter carriers had also been told to bring back cream if they could get it.

The Guiders, Miss Stewart and Miss Nalder, after collecting post-cards from the Company to their home-people to say that they had arrived safely, set off to the village in quest of cocoa and one or two other items they required.

'Bring a newspaper or two,' said Miss Wilson. 'We don't want to miss any news there may be.'

'Can I have some writing-paper?' pleaded Joey. 'I've only got my pad, and I don't want to use it too much.'

'What do you want with writing-paper?' demanded 'Charlie.'

'Keep notes for the *Chaletian*,' said Jo, who, as editor of the School magazine, was sometimes hard put to it for fresh matter. 'I'll take the notes and give them to Stacie to throw into decent shape if I haven't time to do it myself.'

'Very well,' said Miss Stewart. 'Anyone want anything else?'

'Milk chocolate, please,' coaxed Evadne. 'Poppa gave me some, but I guess I left it at home—like the cocoa! Anyway, I can't find it anywhere.'

'Only a small cake, then,' said the captain severely. 'I

don't want you down either bilious or with toothache here.'

Evadne had to console herself with that, though she pulled a long face over it once she was away from the Guiders.

Nobody else appeared to want anything, so the two set off on their three-mile tramp, leaving the camp humming with business. Joey called her band together, and led them away to the forest. Marie called her assistant cooks together, and set them to peeling potatoes over old newspapers, so that the skins might be kept tidily together and, later, burnt in the incinerator. As Juliet said afterwards, it was a peaceful and happy scene when she marched the strawberry-gatherers off to the field. Even the sun was doing his best to brighten things, and the cooks were very thankful that the shade of the pines reached over their trestle-table.

The wood-gatherers were very busy. As none of them could carry a great deal at a time, they were coming to and fro between the forest and the camp, bringing their gleanings in the shape of twigs, branches, and anything that they thought would burn well and help to keep the fire going.

The first sensation was provided by Cornelia Flower, who presently came back to the camp, dragging behind her what looked like a young tree at first sight. She had torn her overall in five places; her fair hair was tangled; her face was covered with green smears, and her bare arms and legs were scratched till she looked as if she had had an encounter with an army of cats.

'*Cornelia!* What have you done to yourself?' exclaimed the captain, who was the first to behold this vision.

Cornelia looked at her burden complacently. Then she glanced down at herself, and her smile was cut short. 'Guess I'm a mite torn,' she said.

'But, my dear girl, what possessed you to try to bring a thing like that?' asked Miss Wilson, as she waved her hand towards it.

'Well, I saw it, and it looked good to me, so I fetched

it,' explained Cornelia in aggrieved tones. 'I thought it would save a bit—a big thing like that.'

'But, Cornelia, it's green wood. Didn't you see that for yourself?' said Miss Wilson gently. 'It won't burn because it's still full of sap. It will only smoke horribly. And how on earth did you manage to tear it down?'

'I didn't. I found it on the ground—I *told* you so just now,' protested Cornelia, an injured look in the enormous blue eyes she raised to the Guider.

'Found it on the ground!' exclaimed Miss Wilson. Then she returned to the task in hand. 'But how *did* you manage to damage yourself so much? You look as if you had been through half a dozen adventures all rolled into one!'

Cornelia stood on one foot, a trick of hers, and rubbed the other up and down her leg. 'Guess I brought it back the shortest way,' she mumbled at length.

Further inquiry elicited the fact that, since some of the paths were too narrow to permit of the great bough being dragged along them in safety, she had simply set her teeth, and come as best she could through bushes, thicket, path, ditch, or anything else that lay in her way. Later in the day, some of them going through the forest, found traces of her journey, and, as Miss Wilson, who was one of the party, said, a tank could scarcely have scattered more destruction.

For the present, she was sent off to make herself presentable, while the captain, arming herself with the only axe in the camp, tried to chop up that bough into convenient lengths, the idea being to keep them beside the fire, so that they might dry. It was a thankless job, for the green wood turned the axe, and Miss Wilson was by no means an expert in this sort of work.

Meanwhile, the rest of the wood-gatherers, profiting by Cornelia's experience, brought armfuls of old stuff, which had only to be laid in the flames to flare up at once. Maria Marani, Lilli van Huysen, and Violet Allison were ordered to pile it tidily, for the gatherers simply tossed it down somewhere near the fire or the incinerator, and left it at that.

Mittagessen was progressing, and Marie was in the act

57

of putting the potatoes into the gently-boiling water in the dixies, when a terrific yell from the woods brought everyone within hearing to her feet, and sent Miss Wilson flying to the trees, her axe still in her hand, her face pale with anxiety.

There came the sound of hurrying feet, and then, through the trees, burst Vanna di Ricci, her face white, her eyes nearly starting out of her head. 'Oh, Madame!' she gasped, as she tripped over a tree-root into Miss Wilson's arms. 'Oh, Madame, Joey has disappeared!'

'What? What do you mean, Vanna?' demanded the captain, setting her on her feet again none too gently. '*How* has Jo disappeared?'

Vanna burst into tears. She had had a bad fright, and Miss Wilson's bracing treatment was the last straw. With a wild look round for aid, the captain set to work to get some sense out of her as quickly as possible. 'Listen, Vanna, you must stop crying. If anything has happened to Jo, tell us what it is, so that we may go to her at once. Come, be brave!'

Vanna gulped, choked over a sob, and then, wiping her eyes on the back of her hand—since she had lost her handkerchief—announced, 'She is swallowed up in the earth.'

A death-like silence followed on this highly dramatic statement. It was broken by the captain, who, clutching her head as if she feared it would burst open, demanded, 'How do you mean? Has she fallen down a hole anywhere?'

'No, Madame,' replied Vanna, rather calmer now than she had been. 'The earth opened, and—and——'

'Don't talk nonsense!' said Miss Wilson shortly. 'We aren't in the earthquake zone here, and if we were, there certainly hasn't been one to-day. How *could* the earth "open and swallow her up?" She must have stepped on a heap of old leaves and pine-needles, drifted over some depression in the ground, and they have given way beneath her weight.'

'But I passed there myself the moment before, Madame,' protested Vanna.

Miss Wilson looked at her, exasperated. Then, feeling

58

that it might be serious, she summoned two or three of those who happened to be in the camp at the time, and, with Vanna to lead, they set out for the place where the contretemps had happened. According to Vanna's story, only got out of her by dint of much questioning, she had been gathering sticks in a little clearing where beech and linden trees grew. She had seen Joey following the path she herself had just quitted, and had called to her. Jo had looked up, and called back—a call that was suddenly changed into a yell of dread as the earth 'opened' beneath her feet, and she disappeared in less than a second, to the horror of Vanna.

'Did you find out what had happened then?' asked the captain.

Vanna shook her head. 'No, Madame. I thought it best to come to you.'

'Although for all you knew, Jo might have broken her leg or her arm, and be lying there helpless or in pain?' It was the only comment the captain made, but Vanna's whiteness vanished under the wave of scarlet that dyed her from throat to forehead.

Nothing more was said till they came to the little clearing, and the unfortunate Vanna, who had returned to her normal colouring, pointed out the place where Joey had so mysteriously vanished. Bidding the girls keep back for the moment, and feeling her way carefully, testing every step she took, Miss Wilson went forward, to stop, just in time, on the brink of a large hole, surrounded at the edges with piled-up dead leaves, pine-needles, pine-cones, and other forest débris. She swirled it about with her axe, in order to discover how much of it had a good foundation, and was rewarded by hearing Jo's voice say, with decided crossness in its tones, 'When you've *quite* done trying to play robin to the babes in the wood, perhaps you'll pull yourself together and help me to get out of this!'

'Joey!' cried the Guider, relief in every accent. 'Are you quite all right, dear? No bones broken or anything?'

Jo declared afterwards that she simply had not recognised Miss Wilson's voice, or she never would have replied as she did, 'For Heaven's sake stop maundering and use your wits and HELP ME TO GET OUT!'

Recognising that there was not much wrong with her but temper, the Guider called out that help would come in a few moments, and wriggled back to where the others stood, clutching at each other fearfully. 'Jo is all right,' she said, as she reached them. 'I think she must have trodden on a pile of leaves, as I said, and it gave way beneath her. If you trod on it first, Vanna, I expect that loosened whatever was holding it together, and Jo's weight would finish the matter. Now we must get her up. It's very dark in there—too dark to see properly. But I should say she is at least ten feet down, so we shall need ropes.—Carla, run back to camp and bring me that length of rope at the side of my tent. Be as quick as you can. Jo isn't hurt—at least, not seriously; but she is certainly very cross.' Her eyes twinkled as she said this, and the girls looked at each other. *What* had Jo been saying?

Carla fled down the path to the camp, and made for the commandant's tent, calling as she went past the camp-fire that Jo was all right but in a hole, so that those who could not leave their duties might be relieved of any anxiety on her account. She found the rope, neatly coiled, by the door of the tent, snatched it up and then tore back.

Miss Wilson took it, and, followed by the three biggest girls, went back to the hole where Joey was. 'Josephine!' she called, using the girl's full name, so that she might guess who it was.

'Miss Wilson! Is that you?' called back Joey. 'I've fallen into some kind of hole, and I can't get out—the walls are too smooth. That ass Vanna must have seen me fall, but she never came near. And a few minutes ago, another idiot came along and asked if I was hurt, and didn't do a thing to help. I do think people are asses!'

Choking back her mirth, the captain crawled a little nearer. 'We've got a rope, Joey. I will let it down, and you must make a noose round your shoulders. Then the rest of us will pull you up. Do you think you can manage?'

'Rather!' said Jo.

'Then look out! Here it comes!'

The rope was swung down, and as it stopped swinging,

Miss Wilson knew that Jo had it safely. 'Running bowline!' she called down. 'Shout when you are ready.' Then she turned to the others. 'Run that end of it round this beech, to give us a purchase. Then heave on that end as hard as you can. It will take us all our time to get Joey to the top, for she will be a dead-weight.'

They did as they were told, and then Jo's call told them that she was ready. They stood by their places on the rope, and Miss Wilson gave the word—'Heave!'

They hove with all their might, for though Jo was slenderly built, she was a good height, and by no means as light as she looked. The perspiration streamed from them as they hauled, and Vanna afterwards declared that she thought her muscles must crack. But at length Jo's hands appeared above the edge of the little pit, grasping at it eagerly. The leaves gave way beneath her clutch, but the rescuers were still pulling vigorously, and she was finally landed, face downwards, on the piled-up rubbish of (it seemed) at least a century, and dragged over it to safer ground. Then they relaxed their efforts, and she struggled to her feet, a wildly dishevelled figure, with her hair full of leaves and pine-needles, a pleasing streak of mud down one cheek, a scratch across the other, her overall fit only for the tub, and wrath in her eyes. She turned to the Guider first. 'Thanks awfully, Miss Wilson. It's a blessing you were here, or I might have stayed there till all hours of the night.'

'Oh, someone would have found you,' said Miss Wilson. 'And now, we'd better go back to camp. I'm sure you would like a bath and fresh clothes!'

Jo looked down at her maltreated overall. 'I do rather need it,' she acknowledged.

'I should think you do!' murmured Vanna.

Like a flash, Jo was down on her. 'And where do *you* come in? What possessed you to run like that? You simply let me go and never came near me. For all *you* knew I might have been dead or dying! There might have been vipers at the bottom of that pit, and if I'd been all black and swollen out when you came back, you'd have looked pretty, wouldn't you? And as for that other idiot who came after you. . . . Which of you was it by the way?' she added, scanning their faces with wrathful curiosity.

Meekly, but with a lack of grammar surprising in a mistress, Miss Wilson owned up. 'I'm very sorry, Jo—but—it was me!'

CHAPTER VIII

JULIET GOES FISHING

IF Jo had set out to create a sensation, she had certainly gone the right way about it. First there had been her sudden disappearance; then she had called the captain an idiot. 'And I might just as well have added "blithering" to it,' she told Frieda that afternoon during siesta-hour. 'I felt like it, goodness knows!'

'It was bad enough as it was,' declared Frieda, choking back a laugh. 'I never saw Miss Wilson at a loss before.'

She took it all right, though,' said Joey, rolling over on her back. 'Bill is a good sport.'

However, that was in the future. At the moment of 'Bill's' confession, the girls stood stock-still, and an electric pause ensued. No one quite knew what to say—Joey least of all. To have told your captain that she was an ass and an idiot, especially when she was also your Science mistress at school was something out of the ordinary.

It was left to Miss Wilson herself to break the silence. Turning to the others, she said in her normal tones, 'Now then, Guides, back to camp! We want to get all the work done this morning. Will someone please see that Cornelia has done as I told her?'

The girls turned and went back, leaving the captain and the heroine of the situation to coil up the rope and come back together. Joey did it in a profound silence, and slung the coil over her shoulder. Miss Wilson watched her with a twinkle in her eyes. She knew that Jo was trying to find words with which to apologise for her involuntary rudeness, and the Guider was inwardly chuckling at the situation.

Presently, as they walked down the path together, Jo's tongue regained its usual freedom. 'I'm awfully sorry, Captain,' she said. 'I didn't think it was you—you know I wouldn't call you names like that, don't you? I thought it was one of the others.'

'Miss Nalder, do you mean? Or did you think it was Miss Stewart?' asked Miss Wilson gravely.

Jo looked at her suspiciously, but not a muscle of 'Bill's' face moved as she made this outrageous suggestion, which the head-girl promptly repelled vehemently. 'Of course not! I thought it was Grizel—or one of the babes. I know it was frightfully discourteous, but I was so furious at being left like that, that I honestly didn't bother *what* I said,' she confessed, with an uneasy wriggle.

'I see,' began Miss Wilson. Then she stopped. 'Joey! Why are you wriggling like that? You haven't been stung by anything, I hope?' There was alarm in her tones. For though she did not for a moment fear the vipers of Jo's pleasing suggestion, she knew that it was quite possible that the girl had been stung by a wasp or a hornet, and both insects could leave an appreciable amount of poison behind them.

'No,' said Jo. 'It's only—well, I must have half a kilo of soil down my neck, I should think; and I keep feeling as though beetles were running over me—and ants.'

'That's easily decided,' said the captain, as they came to the edge of the meadow. 'Go to your tent and undress at once, and put on your swimming-suit. You can take a dip in the lake, and that ought to send far enough any insects you may have garnered.'

Jo fled to the tent thankfully, and presently emerged, clad in her dark-blue swimming-suit, and made for the water at top speed. She came out, looking much better for her dip, and then retired to dry and dress. By the time she was ready, everyone else had got back to camp, including the other two Guiders, and Evadne was distending her cheeks and producing weird noises in a valiant effort to play 'Come to the cook-house door, boys.'

Jo dropped down in her accustomed place on the ground-sheet between Frieda and Simone, with Marie opposite her. These four were old and tried friends of many years' standing, and she knew that, whatever they might feel about her latest exploits, they would wait till they got her alone before they made any comments. As for the rest, with the Guiders there—for the other two had returned from their errand—they couldn't very well say all they were yearning to say. They had to take it out in casting meaning looks at Jo.

Mittagessen passed off without any hitch, however, and while the cooks retired for their siesta at once, as was the due of those who had already borne the heat and burden of the day, the rest set to work to wash up, fold up the ground-sheets and American-cloth, and generally tidy the camp. The fire was damped down with a little of Cornelia's green wood, as well as some dry twigs, so that it would keep going while everyone rested. When the siesta was over, some of them went to practise for their Boatswain's Badge, while the rest went for a 'Nature' walk with the captain. The faithful four settled down on the sandy shore, with a rock at their backs, and one of the huge Japanese parasols belonging to the school for shade. In England there is no need of such things; but in the Tirol, the summer heat is sometimes so intense that to go about without such a protection is to ask for sunstroke. This was a particularly hot day, when the sky was vividly blue, and the sun glared down with a heat that set up a hazy mist over the lake, through which distant objects assumed a wavy outline. The girls were thankful to know that they must not stir for at least an hour, but might take their ease as they chose, so long as they were quiet. It must be confessed that most of them were soon fast asleep. The day had begun early, and had been hot and filled with thrills. They had eaten an excellent meal, and were ready for a rest.

'Sound asleep,' murmured Miss Nalder, as she and Miss Stewart made their way to a spot on the sandy shore which they had marked out for their own. 'There's Joey and her clan—I recognise the "Red Peril." '

Miss Stewart laughed at this reference to the scarlet sunshade which Jo generally took possession of when she needed such a thing.

'Well, you two,' said Miss Wilson from behind their rock at this moment, 'are all the lambs asleep at last?'

'Most of them,' said 'Charlie,' dropping down with a sigh of thankfulness.

'Thank goodness you bagged the green sunshade, Bill, I see the others are all in use.'

'It's not correct, really,' said Miss Nalder seriously. 'A Guide never carries an umbrella, and I'm sure she should never descend to a sunshade—even of the Japanese variety.'

'Guides were first instituted in England,' said Miss Wilson, tossing over a packet of chocolate to her colleagues. 'It's the rarest thing in the world to have heat like this in England. Do you know that the thermometer is at ninety-five degrees in the shade?'

'I didn't look at it, but it feels like it,' yawned Miss Stewart.

Then they settled down with books, as glad of the rest as any of the girls.

Meanwhile, the faithful four were engaged in discussing the events of the morning.

'Joey, how could you call the captain an idiot?' asked Marie.

'I didn't,' said Joey.

'Joey!' It was an exclamation from all three.

'Well—not knowingly, anyway. It was meant for any of you, which I thought it was,' explained Joey somewhat incoherently. 'And you'd have been mad too, if you'd fallen into a messy hole where it was almost pitch-dark, and there were dead leaves and insects and all sorts of creepy-crawlies, and you couldn't get out. I tried, but it was so soft that whenever I put any weight on my fingers, it simply crumbled away. And it was so smooth that there was no hold anywhere. I wasn't exactly afraid, for I knew Vanna had seen me go. But I didn't want to stay there any longer than I could help. And then, to have someone come and yell to ask if I were hurt, when all I wanted was to get out, was the final edge.'

'No one will forget it, my Jo,' said Simone, a smile brightening her usually grave little face. 'It will go down in the School—what do you say?—traditions always.'

65

'Along with all the other mad things that have ever happened—I know!' groaned Jo. 'Even if I ever become a famous writer, most people here will know me as the girl who called the Science mistress an idiot and an ass!'

'Oh, I think they will have more than that by which to remember you,' said Frieda demurely.

'If it weren't so hot, I'd get up and shake you,' retorted her friend. 'As it is, consider it done, please.'

Frieda laughed, and the four, with one consent, rolled over and went to sleep.

The rest of the afternoon was passed as they had arranged, and it was a hot and weary throng that came to *Kaffee und Kuchen* at seventeen o'clock by European time. Carla had stayed in camp to see to it, and with her had been Elisaveta, Cornelia, and two people who tired quickly—Anita Rincini and Maria Marani. They had everything ready when the others returned, and it was served almost as the last straggler reached camp. They lingered over it, chattering about the jolly time they were having, and discussing plans for the next day.

'I think I'll take the boat out and go fishing this evening,' said Juliet presently. 'Fish would make a nice change for breakfast, and if we kill them first, and then fasten them in a basket, and sink it at the water's edge, they'll be beautifully fresh.'

'You can't possibly go, then,' said Miss Nalder. 'Think of the mosquitoes!'

'Bother! I'd forgotten them,' said Juliet.

'Get up early and fish at sunrise,' suggested Jo.

'Yes; I might do that.'

'Are there any fish in the lake, by the way?' asked Grizel.

Everyone turned to Frieda as the one likely to know, and she nodded her head. 'Oh yes! There are trout and some other small fresh-water fish. I have heard that there are pike too, but I have never seen any. Papa and Gottfried have caught the smaller kinds, though, and they taste very good.'

'Then I'll get up at five and see what luck I have,' decided Juliet, who, during a visit to the Irish home of her fiancé, one Donal O'Hara, had become an enthusiastic fisherwoman. 'Anyone coming with me?'

'I will—if I'm awake,' said Jo.

'I'd like to come, too,' added Grizel.

'Very well, then. If Madame says we may, we three will see if we can't give you a treat for breakfast.' She looked at the Guiders, and they nodded.

By all means, go if you like,' said Miss Wilson. 'Don't forget to put on sweaters, though. It will be chilly on the lake at that time. And don't try to drown yourselves, whatever you do.'

'We can all swim,' said Grizel, with a laugh. 'As for Jo, I believe she was born a fish originally.'

Jo grinned at this tribute to her powers, but held her tongue. At the moment she was inclined to efface herself until the effect of her address to Miss Wilson had worn off a little. She need not have been afraid, however. The next morning's fishing expedition was to provide them all with thrills enough to obliterate completely anything she might have done.

It was dawn when the three girls stole out of their tents, clad in swimming-suits, jerseys, and raincoats. The night had been hot, and they felt that they would be thankful if it were only cooler on the water. Juliet carried the fishing-tackle; Jo bore a bugle, for she meant to blow the reveillé from the lake; Grizel had a basket on each arm. One was for the fish, but the other was full.

'What on earth's the use of bringing a full basket?' demanded Jo, as the elder girl deposited her burdens in the boat. 'We want them empty for the fish.'

'Infants and fools,' remarked Grizel.

'What do you mean? I'm neither an infant nor a fool, and I'll thank you to stop your sarcasm!'

'If you two squabble so loudly, you'll disturb the others,' put in Juliet, trying to pour oil on the troubled waters. 'Hop in, Jo.—Come along, Grizel. I quite agree with Jo, by the way,' she added, as they clambered into the boat and she hung over the stern to loose the chain. 'Why *did* you bring that basket?'

'Because I knew we'd all be hungry out on the water,' returned Grizel. 'I made *Kaffee* last night, and put it in a flask. The rest is sandwiches and apricots. *Now* are you both satisfied?'

'What a brain!' said Jo admiringly. 'All right, Griselda. I'll forgive you this time.—Which way do we row, Juliet?'

'Over there to the farther shore,' said Juliet, taking up her oars and standing up in the boat to give them a good shove off. 'There we are!'

The boat went rocking out on to the broad bosom of the lake, where the early rays of the sun were just beginning to strike down, and the girls made good time with their oars till they reached the part they wanted. Then, while Juliet and Jo let down the anchor in case the current should move them, Grizel unpacked her basket, and they were soon enjoying the sandwiches and coffee with good appetites. The apricots followed, and then Juliet brought out her lines and proceeded to bait the hooks for them.

'How dark the water is here!' remarked Joey, peering down at the black depths. 'Are you sure this is the best place, Juliet?'

'I asked at the farm when I went there for milk last night,' said Juliet. 'They told me it was generally possible to get a good catch hereabouts.'

The three lines went over the side of the boat, and the girls sat quietly, talking in undertones at intervals. For twenty minutes or so they caught nothing, and Jo the impatient was about to suggest their rowing farther along, when Grizel uttered an exclamation, and began to haul in her line.

'Gently—gently! You'll lose it if you tug like that,' said Juliet, coming to her assistance.

A moment later, the catch was over the side of the boat and being disengaged from the hook by the elder girl. It was some kind of trout, about half a pound in weight. Juliet sighed for her rod and line; but fishing with it would have been difficult here, for she did not know the water; so they had to be content with their ordinary lines. Grizel was very proud of her capture, and Jo, for once, refrained from trying to take her down a peg. Besides, her own line called for her attention in a few seconds, and after that, they were kept busy for some time.

Presently, since the catch seemed to be ending, Juliet suggested that they should up anchor, and try again farther along. They had not nearly enough to satisfy the appetites of the camp, and it would be difficult to choose who should eat fish and who should not.

They did as she suggested, and were rewarded by further good hauls. Finally when the two baskets were full to overflowing, and they had enough to give everyone a good breakfast of fish, Juliet suggested that they had better return. The camp was awake and at work now, for they could see the busy figures on the other shore. Whistles and bugle-calls rang out, and Jo remembered, much to her chagrin, that she had forgotten to blow reveillé. Then a darker patch in the water caught her eye. 'Let's have a shot over there,' she pleaded. 'I should love to catch a pike, if I could!'

'Thanks! I'd rather be excused,' said Juliet, nevertheless doing as she wished. 'Don't you know that pike are known as "fresh-water sharks," Jo? They are the fiercest fresh-water fish known.'

'Still, I'd like to be able to say I'd caught one,' argued Jo.

Above the dark patch they anchored once more, and the three lines were thrown out again. Grizel caught two more little fish, and Joey got one which was quite the biggest they had taken.

Juliet did nothing, and was just about to suggest that they really must go back, when she suddenly felt a tug at her line. 'A bite!' she cried. Very carefully she began to draw in; and then it struck her that whatever she had caught this time was considerably larger than anything which had gone before.

'Whatever can it be?' asked Grizel.

'I bet it's a pike,' said Jo, who was leaning perilously far over the side of the boat. 'I believe I can just see it down there—like a shadow.—Juliet, it's *huge*! Whatever it is, it's simply enormous!'

Juliet had no breath left which to answer. She was bending all her energies to drawing in this mysterious catch. The wet line was cutting across her hands, and her muscles felt like cracking. The other two lent a hand at this point, and slowly—very slowly—they pulled it in. Gradually it neared the surface—a long, dark object, wider at one end than the other. Suddenly, as it swayed in the water, the three girls caught sight of its face.

There was a united scream, which brought most of the Guides on the opposite shore to the water's edge at a run. Then a splash, and the next minute they were furiously struggling with the anchor, hauling it up anyhow and with little heed as to what happened. The boat heeled over dangerously for a moment; Then, as Grizel, who had kept her head better than the others, flung her weight on the opposite side, it slowly righted. The next moment the anchor was aboard and they were rowing as if sharks pursued them.

'What *can* have happened?' exclaimed Miss Stewart, who had joined the Guides on the shore.

'Something must have frightened them,' said Miss Nalder, who had caught a glimpse of the white face of Grizel as the latter turned her head to see that they were heading for the right spot. 'Frieda, run for the captain.'

Frieda turned and ran, and came back with Miss Wilson just as the boat grounded. Its three occupants stayed where they were—Joey, indeed, was very sick at the moment—and they had to be helped out.

'What has happened?' asked the captain anxiously, as she slipped an arm round Juliet's waist and supported to a rock where she could sit down. 'What is the matter, Juliet?'

With chattering teeth Juliet tried to answer. After a moment she succeeded. 'Oh, captain, there's a dead body in the water over there, and I—HOOKED—IT!'

CHAPTER IX

AN UNEXPECTED CATCH

IF Jo had created a sensation the previous day, Juliet's effort simply outdid it. There was deathly silence while everyone stared at her. Even Miss Stewart, who was holding Jo (who had collapsed limply as soon as she was moved, and looked more dead than alive), stared vacantly. Grizel, now she was on land, was managing to keep her feet, but she was the only one to do so.

Finally, Vanna spoke. 'But *no*!' she said, in her own pretty Italian.

Juliet was past speaking now. The memory of the waxen face with its floating tresses of golden hair, of which she had caught a glimpse before she had flung away her line, was too much for her. Grizel replied for her. 'It's true enough,' she asserted. 'We all three saw it—over there, where we were fishing last.'

At this moment Simone Lecoutier, who had just come from the forest where she had been gathering wood for the fire, saw Jo, and, flinging her armful of twigs in all directions, tore to the rescue, 'But what, then, had happened to Jo?' she demanded as she caught one cold, clammy hand in hers. 'Oh, she is ill—she is terribly ill!'

Thus recalled to the condition of the girls, Miss Wilson took charge. 'Take Jo to my tent,' she said sharply to Miss Stewart. 'She ought to be got to bed as soon as possible.'

At this, Jo opened her eyes. 'No!' she said, with as much emphasis as she was capable of producing in her present extremity. 'I *won't* be alone.' A fresh spasm of sickness overtook her at this moment, but when it was over she repeated her words. 'Not alone! I won't go anywhere alone . . . not after . . . *that*! Take me . . . to . . . the fire!'

Miss Stewart lifted her up from the sand on which she had laid her down and, with a strength amazing to behold, carried the girl over to the fire, and deposited her on the grass beside it. 'Carla, go to my tent,' she said to the young Tirolean, who was busily stoking up, for, since Jo had begged for warmth, she must have it. 'In my case you will find a small flask. Bring it here.'

Carla ran off, and presently returned with the flask. Miss Stewart unscrewed the top, poured out a small dose of brandy, and literally forced it down Jo's throat.

Whether it was the spirit or the fact that she had fought against it—Joey hated all spirits with a deadly hatred— the head-girl sat up a moment or two later, looking decidedly more like herself. 'Sorry to have been—a nuisance,' she said feebly.

'All right,' said 'Charlie,' laying her back again, and throwing over her a light rug which someone had brought. 'You had better take things easily for a few minutes or so.'

Jo lay back thankfully, the colour coming back to her cheeks.

Presently Grizel came up and sat down beside her. 'Better?' she asked, in an off-hand manner.

'Yes, thanks,' said Jo. 'Where's Juliet?'

'Over there on the shore. Charlie's dosing her with brandy.'

Jo closed her eyes and lay still. But a few minutes more brought Juliet to them, assisted by the captain, and looking rather better now. 'You—you'll do something about it, captain, won't you?' she asked.

'I'm going to send a message to Herr Semmering at the farm,' said Miss Wilson briskly. 'He will know what it is best to do. Meanwhile, you three had best go to one of the tents and go to bed for a while. A sleep will do you all good.'

'I don't feel as if I could ever sleep again,' said Jo, who had sat up now and was leaning against Frieda, who had come over to them.

'Nonsense!' said the captain crisply. 'You've had brandy, haven't you?'

'Quarts of it, if my throat's anything to go by!'

'Then you'll soon find that you go to sleep. Brandy is a soporific.'

Jo shook her head feebly; but it was obvious that she

was rapidly recovering from the shock of what they had seen.

'Come along; some of the others have been putting your beds right,' said the captain, giving the head-girl a hand, and helping her to her feet. 'Can you walk, Jo?'

'Yes, thank you,' replied Jo.

She was glad, however, of the arm Miss Wilson slipped round her waist, and thankful to lie down as soon as she was in her pyjamas. Grizel and Juliet were already there, and when the last of the trio was safely settled, 'Bill' pulled the tent-flap across the doorway and left them. Ten minutes later, Miss Nalder stole over the grass and peeped in. The brandy had done its work, and all three were fast asleep.

'The best thing possible for them,' said Miss Wilson, when she was told. 'Meanwhile, I hope those men will hurry up and begin dragging operations. I should be thankful if it were all over before the girls woke again.'

'And, meanwhile,' added 'Charlie,' joining them with a huge enamel jug in either hand, 'we have to keep the others off the topic if we can. I suppose it really *has* happened? They aren't just suffering from the results of reading thrillers?'

'It happened all right,' said the captain. 'Jo and Juliet aren't usually sick for nothing. I am going to forbid any chatter about it. The sooner we manage to forget, the better. It it were only possible to find a good camping place elsewhere, I would strike camp and move to-day. As we can't, we must just carry on, and try to keep their minds off the subject.' With this, she left the others, to pounce on Elsie Carr, who was running past, barefoot, and demanded where her shoes were.

By the time Elsie had been sent to her tent to get them, *Frühstück* was ready, and the girls were summoned as quietly as possible. 'Bill' said grace, and then, before the girls sat down, she gave them a brief command to say nothing about the early morning's happenings. 'You are not to discuss it at all,' she said. 'I wish you to forget it as far as possible. Herr Semmering and his men will come shortly, and will drag for what Juliet fished up, and we shall all be far too busy to attend to them. Remember, girls, not a word. If I hear anyone talking about it, I will send her home as soon as it can be arranged.'

At this dire threat one or two people closed their lips firmly. They were, of course, thrilled by the event; but they did not wish to be sent home in disgrace just after camp had opened. 'Bill' had put an effectual stop to all gossip about it, and when, breakfast over, they set to work to clear up, no one so much as breathed the word 'fishing.'

Roll-call and inspection took place as usual, the sleeping three never moved throughout the time. The wood-gatherers, in charge of Carla von Flügen, went off to the forest to collect their daily burden. The cooks busied themselves with the meal for the day; and those detailed to go for butter and milk went with Miss Nalder. This was a wise precaution, for when they reached the farm they found good Frau Semmering all agog to discuss the tragedy, and none of the Guides would have been able to deal with her. Miss Nalder, whose round, rosy face and innocent, child-like air were most misleading, as a good many of the more wicked middles had discovered, easily checked the excellent women's torrent of words, and the girls returned to camp, leaving her no wiser than she had been before.

At half-past eleven, Frieda, peeping into the tent, came back to announce that Joey and Grizel were awake, and wanted to know if they might get up. 'Jo says she is very hungry,' said Frieda, carefully suppressing Jo's more emphatic remark. 'She asks if she may have breakfast.'

'Very well, Frieda. Tell them to take their clothes to another tent and dress there. Juliet had better have her sleep out.'

Frieda ran off, and while the pair were dressing, Simone and she prepared a dainty little breakfast for them. There was no fish—not a girl in the camp would look at them, and they had all been cast into the incinerator. But the *Kaffee* was good, and stronger than usual; the crusty rolls were thickly buttered; Simone made a delicious little *omelette aux fines herbes* in her best style, and it was a dainty little meal that awaited them when they finally emerged, looking much better for their extra sleep.

'Omelette? That's you, Simone, of course!' said Jo. 'You dear!'

Soft colour flushed Simone's sallow little face, and a world of adoration filled her eyes at the words. 'I liked doing it,' was all she said.

'Well, if it tastes as good as it smells,' remarked Grizel, 'it will be nectar and ambrosia mixed. You are a jolly good cook, Simone—I'll say that for you!'

The omelette soon disappeared, and it was while the girls were washing up their utensils that there came the solemn tread of heavily-booted feet, and the farmer and his men appeared among the trees. Miss Wilson saw them first, as she was giving lessons in Morse signalling to a party of junior Guides. She at once dismissed her class, and went forward to greet the men.

'And—where the corpse was found,' said Herr Semmering, a big, fair man with a goodnatured, stupid face, '—can the well-born young lady come and show me where it lies?'

'I am sorry,' said Miss Wilson, 'but she is, at present, very poorly as a result of the shock, and is in bed.'

'Ach! Then how do we go?' he asked.

'I think I can show you myself,' she said, though with a little inward shudder at the thought of rowing over the dark, calm water which concealed so hideous a thing. 'It is in that dark patch over there—near the farther shore.'

His eyes widened. 'There? But—gracious lady——'

'Well? What is it?' asked Miss Wilson, a little impatiently, as he came to a halt.

'I should have said—it is there that the pike feed,' he stammered.

One of the men, who had been listening carefully, now put in *his* word. 'Pardon, gracious lady, but is—it—a man or a woman?'

'A woman—at least, it had long, golden hair, so the girls told me,' replied the captain.

'A woman?' He turned to the others. 'But there is no woman missing these five years. And it cannot be Grete Steidhahl, for she was dark.'

'At least, she is there,' said Miss Wilson, who was beginning to wonder if they meant to get to work that day at all.

'Well, it is not Grete Steidhahl,' grunted the farmer. 'I can tell you *that*.' He turned to the aggravated captain. 'It is of a niece of my own that we speak, gracious lady. She disappeared one day, and has never been seen again. —But I know that she is well, Auguste. I had a visit from her husband last month—the young French artist. He came to close his *loge*, and take away all he needed. The rest he destroyed. They will not return here, for he has got on in the world, and neither he nor Grete wishes to remember that she comes of poor farming-folk like us.'

'Horrid little snob!' commented Miss Wilson mentally. Then she returned to the matter in hand. 'I am glad, Herr Semmering, that this is not your niece. But if not she, it is some poor woman who has met perhaps, with an accident. Will you not hasten with your work?'

The farmer nodded, and climbed over the fence, followed by his men. 'As you say, *gnädiges Fräulein*, it would be well to begin. You have boats?'

Miss Wilson indicated the boats, and he made for them, followed by the eye of every girl in the camp. 'Girls, get on with your duties till I return,' she said, before she got into a light, collapsible skiff, and, with a swift stroke, swung out into the sunshine of the lake.

The fierceness of her tones set the girls scurrying off, and Joey and Grizel, who had seen her go, with one accord finished washing up their mugs and plates, and then fled into the forest to help the wood-gatherers.

'I've had enough of it,' said Jo. 'Come on! Let's try down there, and see if we can get some fir-cones for tonight.'

The captain paddled out to the dark patch which Grizel had pointed out to her early that morning, when they had returned in that headlong flight, and waved a hand at it. 'This, *mein Herr*, is the patch of which the young ladies told me. It was here that they received the so-to-be-regretted shock,' she informed him, in German, of course.

He nodded, but the puzzled look came again to his face. 'It is certainly here that the pike feed,' he murmured.

'You will not need me?' queried Miss Wilson, preparing to return to the farther shore.

'I will call you when we have got her,' he said amiably.

'Bill' shuddered violently, and, then, turning her boat, shot back to camp, where she resummoned her Morse class, and set the girls to 'flag-wagging' as hard as ever she could. In another corner of the meadow, 'Charlie' was demonstrating to a chosen few the correct method of making a 'Turk's-Head,' and Miss Nalder was demonstrating camp cookery, in which she was an adept, to an eager set. Joey, who, in consideration of what had happened, had been excused any violent exercise of either strength or brain, was curled up under the Red Peril, bringing the log-book up to date; and Grizel was rearranging the first-aid box, since she had found it looking as though it had been in a cyclone and got the worst of it. 'Those middles are the limit for untidiness,' she grumbled, as Jo paused in her writing to consider her last paragraph. 'Just look at this! Bandages unrolled—sticking-plaster everywhere —iodine bottle set in upside down—it's a wonder they had the sense to cork it tightly!—and everything in a mess!'

'Why don't you find out who did it, and set *her* to tidying it?' asked Jo.

'Because if you want a thing well done, it's advisable to do it oneself,' replied Grizel, rewinding a bandage as she spoke. 'How is that log going?'

'Well, it's eventful, if it's nothing else,' replied Jo, with a grin. 'I wonder how Juliet is?'

'Much better, thank you,' replied Juliet herself, as she came up behind them. 'What are you doing there, Griselda?'

'Making this look like a Guide first-aid box,' said Grizel. 'Yes; you look better, my dear. They're busy out there now,' and she gave a jerk of her head in the direction of the lake.

'Don't speak of it!' said Juliet, with a shudder. 'I never want to go fishing again!'

'I feel rather that way myself,' acknowledged her friend.

'Never mind; come and sit down under the Red Peril, and tell us some more about Ireland.' But before Juliet could do so, a shout from the lake told them that the men had found something.

The entire camp stopped what it was doing to look up. The next moment they were hard at work again. Only Miss Wilson, signalling rapidly to her band, kept one eye on the people in the boat. If they showed any signs of bringing their catch over to the camp she was going to send the girls into the woods at once. She considered that they had had more than enough excitement for one day. But whatever it was, it was not the thing they were expecting, so she turned back and made an effort to disentangle a perfect hurricane of dots and dashes which Paula von Rothenfels was sending her, and which might have been Sanskrit for all she could make of it. 'Send that message again, Paula,' she said sharply. 'You are not allowing sufficient length of time for your dashes.'

Thus adjured, Paula began again, and this time the captain was able to make out the sentence: 'We have had an accident. Send stretcher-bearers at once.' At least, that is what Paula *meant* to say. What it actually read was: 'We have had a message. Send sandwiches at once.'

'There is no sense in that, Paula!' she said crossly. 'Try again and, for goodness' sake, keep your mind on what you are doing.'

'Yes, Madame,' said Paula meekly, as she disentangled her flag which had wrapped itself round its pole.

What more might have been said, no one will ever know, for at that moment, Joey, who had glanced up, squeaked excitedly, 'They've got IT!'

Sure enough, the captain saw the men lifting something which looked like a body into the boat. The next moment she could not believe her ears. Across the still water came the sound of hearty guffaws of laughter.

Miss Stewart heard them too, and dropped her 'Turk's-Head' to come racing across the meadow to her superior officer. 'Madame, what on earth has happened?' she cried. 'Could—could the girls have possibly been mistaken, do you think?'

'We *weren't*!' cried Jo indignantly, as she came up, followed by the rest of the camp. 'We saw it all right. I'm not sick for nothing as a rule! And I must say I think it's horrid of them to laugh at a poor creature——'

'They're rowing for here!' Miss Nalder interrupted her.

The captain opened her lips to order the girls to march off to the forest; but she was checked by a hail from the boat. Leaving the other two to look after the Guides, she went down to the water's edge and called to know what had happened.

'We have got her, *gnädiges Fräulein,*' bellowed good Herr Semmering. 'I am sorry the young ladies had such a fright for nothing—as you will see when we land.'

'Fright for nothing!' repeated Grizel furiously. 'I'm glad he calls it that! The man must be completely hardened— a callous creature!'

'Wait, Grizel,' said Miss Wilson. 'Evidently it is not what you three thought it was. I quite agree that you had a nasty fright; but there may be some explanation of it.'

By this time the boat had reached the shore, and the men were clambering out. Two of them reached land, and then Herr Semmering put his arms under what looked like a girl with flowing golden locks, clad in a dress, dark and sodden with water. He lifted her and handed her over to the two on land. They carried her up the sand and laid her down on it. Then the good farmer beckoned to Miss Wilson. She went very gingerly, for she had no idea what it was she was going to see. The farmer addressed her as she neared them, speaking in rapid, rumbling German, which the rest were too far off to distinguish. They saw Miss Wilson stare; then go nearer and bend over the still figure at the edge of the sand. The next moment she buried her head in her hands and the clear sound of her laughter rang out.

The Guides were aching to go, but Miss Stewart and Miss Nalder still restrained them till the captain, lifting her head, called in tones wobbly with mirth, 'Let them— come!'

They came at top speed, and when they were assembled she made a little sign to the men, and they stood back from the 'body.' The girls looked. Then they gasped. Finally, they too burst out laughing. It was no poor corpse that was before them, but a lay-figure, to the head of which—as they discovered later—had been glued a

79

golden wig. It had been clothed in robes of blue velvet, and had evidently been bundled into the lake just as it was. Herr Semmering was able to explain, when they had all calmed down a little, what must have happened. A letter, sent to one Monsieur Monet, brought a confimatory answer the following week.

When Monsieur Monet, the French artist with whom Grete Steidhahl had run away, had cleared up his *loge* in the previous month, he had been puzzled what to do with the old lay-figure he had been using. He did not want it, for he had a much better one in his Parisian studio, and he considered it would be waste of money to take it back. He had not the time to stay and see it burnt, and he felt that to cast it out and leave it would be to run the risk of giving some child who might stumble over it a fright. He had therefore done what seemed the best thing he could do—lugged it down to the lake and pushed it in at the deep part, never dreaming that the very thing he was trying to avoid would come to pass. He had seen no reason for telling anyone what he had done, and the entire countryside had been in ignorance of it until Juliet's dramatic discovery that morning. By the time the letter had come, however, everyone near had heard of it, and the camp had been pestered nearly out of their lives by visitors and audiences, who all came to stare at them, and comment audibly on them—not always. to their credit, either.

However, that was a week ahead. At the moment the girls shrieked with laughter, even the three who had such a trying experience. But Jo was merely voicing the feelings of all when she finally recovered from her mirth to say disgustedly, 'And we were sick, and were sent to bed, and made to drink horrid brandy, and treated like invalids just for a stupid artist and his even stupider lay-figure!'

Miss Stewart hastened to point the moral. 'That is what comes of reading so many detective novels,' she said. 'If you'd leave thrillers alone, all of you, and try something sensible, you wouldn't be so ready to look for the worst before it happened.'

And, as the stew for dinner boiled over at that moment, the last word lay with 'Charlie.'

CHAPTER X

SATURDAY VISITORS

WEDNESDAY and Thursday having been, as pretty Anne Seymour remarked, full of thrills, it was just as well that Friday was a quiet day. It is true that Giovanna Donati tripped up into a bed of stinging-nettles, from which she was rescued weeping loudly and with face and arms well covered with white blisters; but ammonia soon cured the worst of her ills, and her sobs were silenced by Margia's disgusted remark, 'What a baby!' 'Bill,' who struggled at intervals with Cornelia's green sapling, slipped her wrist, and cut herself; but luckily, the cut was not serious, and 'Charlie' ministered to her with iodine and bandages, so there was little harm done.

Apart from these events, nothing of any consequence took place. On Friday the Guides carried out their projected programme, attending the camp duties in the morning, taking a siesta in the afternoon, and after *Kaffee* at sixteen o'clock, tramping to Weisshalt, the village of Gottlieb Strönen, and spending a happy hour inspecting the little church with its churchyard, and seeing the hut where, so history tells us, he was born. Rufus came with them, Miss Wilson staying at the camp with Maria Marani, Elisaveta, and Violet Allison to look after things, while Juliet, who wanted to finish a letter to her fiancé, finally decided to keep them company.

The rest went off, and returned four hours later, very weary, very hungry, and clamouring loudly for *Abendessen*. They were so tired, that there was no singsong that night. 'Bill' and Grizel took the two sets of Prayers; the flag was lowered; and, all standing together, sang 'Taps.'

'Day is done; gone the sun,
From the sea, from the hills, from the sky.
All is well; safely rest.
God is nigh.'

That over, the Guides retired to bed, and were soon
slumbering sweetly—greatly to the disappointment of the
inhabitants of the district, who crept up as usual in
anticipation of the nightly concert to which they were becoming accustomed.

Reveillé brought them to their feet, refreshed by the
long sleep, and ready for anything.

'Visitors this afternoon,' said the captain, as they sat
at *Frühstück*. 'We must work this morning, so that everything may be as smart as possible.'

'Aren't some of them coming for *Mittagessen*?' asked
Grizel.

'Yes, Dr Jem is, and Dr Jack Maynard. The rest are
coming later. Madame didn't want to have the babies here
all day, and she didn't want to leave Stacie so long.'

'Poor old Stacie!' said Jo, as she demolished the last
of her grape-fruit.

'It's hard lines having to be left out of all the fun like
this!'

'We must hope she may have it next summer,' said
Frieda.

'It will be *your* last summer-term,' Evadne reminded
her. 'And yours, Jo!'

'So it will be! Oh! How I *hate* growing up!' And Jo
groaned deeply.

'But you'll be coming to *me* then,' the Princess reminded her reproachfully. 'Don't you want that, Joey? *I'm*
longing for it.'

'We may all be dead by that time,' said Jo pessimistic-
ally.

'Jo! That's a nice spirit for a Guide!' said the captain
sharply.

'Well, I can't help it. I loathe the idea of growing up,
and I don't care who knows it! I'd much rather remain
as I am!' Jo eyed the rolls thoughtfully. 'Do you think
those rolls would get up and walk if I whistled to them?'

'Oh, I beg your pardon, Joey!' cried Marie, who was nearest, and she made a long arm for the basket. Unfortunately she forgot her coffee which was at the edge of the American-cloth, and over it went, streaming in every direction. 'Oh, I am so sorry!' she cried, as she dived for a cloth to mop up the mess.

'It is a very good thing it is not one of our cloths at school,' remarked Simone, as she came to the rescue, and, together, they righted matters again. 'And here is your roll, Joey.'

'Thank you,' replied Jo, as she accepted it. 'It's really I who ought to say "sorry," you know,' she went on. 'It was my fault in the beginning.'

'We'll take it all as read,' put in Miss Wilson hastily. 'Hurry up, girls, and finish your meal. We are late to-day.'

After *Frühstück*, washing-up. Then came the general tidying of the tents, and shelves, ready for inspection. Every scrap of paper or débris was put into the incinerator; the commissariat-tent was set in perfect order; the American-cloths were wiped down and carefully dried; big loads of firewood were stacked in readiness; and the fire carefully rebuilt. Then the girls raced to their tents to adjust hair and overalls. They could not be expected to wear the uniform, for the weather was still continuing hot, and, early as it was, the thermometer already registered ninety-eight degrees in the shade, with every prospect of going higher as the day wore on. But Guide overalls are neat when properly adjusted, and they looked a very smart, capable set as they stood in their patrols, waiting for the captain to make her rounds. The six cadets—Joey, Grizel, Juliet, Frieda, Simone, and Marie—stood at one side. The four patrols stood at right angles to them, led by Vanna, Carla, Bianca, and Eva, each carrying the patrol flag. On either side of the little mound was set the company flag, and the flag of the Tirol. The captain and her two officers saluted the girls smartly, and then went the rounds, and it is on record that, on this occasion, every patrol was at topmost pitch. Not one bad mark had to be recorded. Even Rufus had had the brass plate on his harness polished, and his coat shone with a burnish which told of the grooming he had received before *Frühstück*.

'Excellent, Guides!' said the captain, when it was all over. 'Now for Prayers!'

Prayers over, the girls scattered to see to *Mittagessen*. Doctors Jem and Jack were a critical pair, and they had no idea of laying themselves open to sarcasm.

'Cold chicken to-day,' said Juliet, who had stewed over the fire the morning before, cooking those same chickens. 'Who makes the salads?'

'The Lilies are responsible for that,' replied the captain. 'The Corn-flowers are to gather the strawberries for dessert, and Grizel will go with you, as Juliet must oversee the arrangements for *Mittagessen*.—Poppies, I want you to be responsible for *Kaffee und Kuchen*. Have what you like; but remember, it's going to be broiling hot, and be merciful to us.—Roses, I'm afraid we shall need far more wood than that. You had better go and see what you can collect. Jo and Carla will be responsible for you; and Frieda and Simone must see to the Poppies.—Miss Nalder, will you come with me to the village for our oddments? There will be the mail to collect, too.—Has anyone any letters to post? Who wants stamps? Oh, and you may each buy a few sweets for to-morrow, if you like.'

There was a stampede for purses as she gave the signal for dismissal, and presently she was at the door of her own tent, writing down various commissions and collecting letters for posting. At length all was ready, and the two Guiders went off chatting cheerfully. They knew that the two doctors would meet them in the village, and bring them back in their car.

As they reached the turn in the path which took them out of sight of the camp, they stopped and looked back on the scene of cheerful bustle. Laughter and song reached them from the Guides, and there were smiles everywhere.

'How happy they are!' laughed Miss Nalder, as they went on their way. 'In spite of all the happenings, they are having a splendid time!'

'Aren't they?' smiled 'Bill.'

'And they all look so well, too! It mayn't be the correct thing to do, but I must admit I feel inclined to pat ourselves on the back for our bonny, healthy, happy set of girls.'

'You aren't any prouder of them than I am,' said Miss Wilson, as they left the forest and struck out down the white road. 'Ouf!! Isn't it hot? I wonder where the mercury will be by noon?'

'Soaring into the hundreds,' declared Miss Nalder, mopping her hot face. 'Well, at least we can know that the girls are comfortable enough. The shade lasts till thirteen over there. And we can retire to the forest when the visitors come if it continues unbearably hot. Is the Robin coming, do you know?'

'I doubt it,' said Miss Wilson. 'They have to be very careful with her, you know, and I don't expect for an instant that Dr Jem will permit it. The long journey and the heat combined would wear her out.'

'Oh, but she'd be in the car most of the way,' objected Miss Nalder.

'There's the climb down from the Sonnalpe, though,' replied Miss Wilson quickly. 'It will be a good thing when they get that electric railway done. Even going by the road at the other end is fairly strenuous.'

Strolling along and talking gaily, they reached the village at length, and promptly made for the little *Gasthaus*, where they cooled down over lemon-sodas. Then they went down the village street to the little post-office, which was also the only shop. There they bought their stamps and chocolate and darning-wool, and one or two other small items.

'Those men ought to be here soon now,' said Miss Wilson, as she gathered up her parcels, and made for the door, after a smiling *'Grüss Gott, meine Frau!'* to the fat, jolly Tirolean who had served them.

'There's a car down the road,' said Miss Nalder, pointing. 'Do you think it can be theirs?'

'I expect so.' Miss Wilson laid down her parcels and shaded her eyes to look down the road at the black speck which was coming rapidly nearer. Five minutes more proved it to be indeed the two doctors; they pulled up at once on seeing the Guiders, and jumped out.

'Well, everything all right?' demanded Dr Jem, as he took the parcels and stowed them away under the seats.

'Quite all right,' said the captain. 'We have had a stirring time; but I don't think anyone is the worse for it. Is Madame coming later with the babies?'

'She's coming, and bringing Gisela and Wanda with her,' replied Dr Jem. 'But it's far too hot for any of the babies; they're to be left at home. The Robin was rather upset about it; but she's a good little soul, bless her, and she made no fuss when we explained that they must all stay at home this Saturday. Perhaps if it's cooler next week, we may bring her and the twins along.'

'Are Gisela and Wanda actually leaving their precious children?' laughed Miss Nalder, as she got into the car.

'Yes; they are very anxious to see the camp, and this is Wanda's last chance. Friedel has been moved to Salzburg, and she must go to him there. It won't be anything like so hot as Vienna, so I told her she might go. They will live outside, Friedel says. He has secured one of the new houses on the slopes of the Mönchsberg, and there are trees all round, so they will have plenty of shade.'

Miss Wilson nodded. She, like everyone else, was very fond of lovely Wanda von Glück, once Wanda von Eschenau, and sister of Marie von Eschenau. And Gisela Mensch had never lost close touch with the Chalet School, for her marriage to Frieda's brother had brought her to the Sonnalpe, which was so near to Briesau am Tiernsee.

'Are they all ready for us?' asked Dr Jack Maynard, brother of a former mistress in the school, and a great friend of everyone.

'Quite ready. I expect you will receive a rousing welcome,' laughed 'Bill.' 'Go slowly, please, or we may miss the opening, and then we shall have to go back.'

'I wonder you dared to leave those young monkeys alone,' he said teasingly. 'And what did you mean by saying you'd been having stirring times?'

'It's too long a story for now,' said the captain, with a twinkle. 'I'll tell you all about it after *Mittagessen*—that is, if the girls don't get first innings. No; it's no use teasing, for neither of us will say a word. Tell me if you have heard from Mollie since we've been away? You have? How is she getting on? Does she see anything of Miss Carthew—I mean, Mrs Cowley?'

'I brought the letter with me,' he said kindly. 'I knew I'd be surrounded by a howling mob—oh, I don't mean you!—as soon as I got there. I'll give it to you to read, and you can let me have it back when camp is over.'

'Stop, Dr Jem!' cried Miss Nalder at this point. 'We have to turn off here. And I don't know if even then you can get the car to camp,' she added.

The path at this point was a much broader one than that which the Guides used, but farther from the camp. The light car easily ran along it for some distance, but at length they were obliged to leave it, as it could go no farther.

'Is it safe?' asked Dr Russell doubtfully.

'I should think so,' said Miss Wilson. 'I can't imagine that anyone here would touch it.'

'I think I'll just lock the steering-column—I've brought the padlock,' he added.

'This is something new, isn't it?' asked the captain, as they waited while he made all secure.

He nodded. 'Herr Doktor Eitel von und zu—I forget the rest, but it's a lovely name for a cheque, I can assure you! Well, he wrote to me about that new treatment they're trying out in Vienna, and most of his letter was a new version of the Book of Lamentations. Motor-thieves are about, and his "Isotta" has gone. He advised me to be very careful of my car—and, as you can see, I am!!'

'At the same time,' put in Dr Maynard, as they turned to walk the remaining distance, 'I can't imagine any self-respecting car-thief going off with that rattler of yours.'

'It's no beauty, I know,' said Jem, with a complacent glance back at the somewhat battered vehicle which lay stranded in a little clearing; 'but she can go when she's put to it.'

'And what is Madame coming in?' demanded Miss Nalder, as they neared the camp.

'Friedel von Glück came yesterday, and he's bringing the girls,' explained Jack Maynard. 'I say, I thought you said we'd get a rousing welcome. Where is it, I'd like to know?'

The two Guiders stared round the camp site. When they had left, it had been a scene of happy activity. Now, not a soul was in sight but themselves. On the fire was a dixie, which appeared, judging by the sounds, to be boiling over. Half-set sheets of American-cloth showed that preparations for *Mittagessen* had been under way. Someone had flung down an armful of branches in a heap near one of the tents. And mingling with the sounds of the boiling water was a strange humming and buzzing, which suddenly grew louder. It was Dr Jem who recognised what was wrong.

'Quick—fly!' he cried, grabbing Miss Wilson and pulling her after him. 'Those are hornets! Someone has roused up a nestful, and the girls are under cover!'

With wild shrieks, the two Guiders were towed down the path to where the car stood. They had just reached it, when Jem Russell stood stock-still. He remembered that he had locked the steering-column, and short of taking her on a lorry or taking her down altogether, there was no means of moving her until he had got that column unlocked. Could he possibly do it in time? With one final leap he reached the car, fumbling in his pocket for the key. It was the last one he got out, of course, and by that time the hornets were very near. 'Fling the women in!' he yelled to Jack Maynard, as he stuck the key into the lock and turned desperately.

Miss Wilson leaped in nimbly, pulling her skirt over her head. Jack Maynard tossed in Miss Nalder beside her, and scrambled in himself. At that moment the engine began to grunt, and the car began to move. Slowly they went at first, then faster and faster, till finally they were flying over the ground, rocking in a way that made the captain wonder, when it was all over, how on earth she had avoided being sick. They crashed out of the forest, still hunted by that humming, angry cloud, and tore down the road, full speed ahead. It was wonderful what that battered, disreputable automobile could do, once it was put to it. Before long they had outdistanced the hornets, and

Jem, meeting a farmer by the way, drew up, and told him.

'We have here the syringes and gas for them, noble Herr,' said the man, showing some cylinders and a couple of fearsome-looking syringes. 'There are too many hornets about this year. This is a new invention, which we have already used with much success. We will go and kill them.' With this he moved off, followed by his men, and Jem, after giving him time to complete the annihilation of the enemy, turned round and drove back.

The hornets were all lying, dead or dying, and the farmer and his men were finishing their work. 'All gone, as you see, noble Herr,' he said, accepting, with a grin, the money Dr Russell slipped into his hand.

'Good!' said Jem. He turned to the others. 'Now we had better get back to the camp and see how many need first-aiding.'

'Also,' added the captain severely, 'who was responsible for this.'

'At least we had a *warm* welcome,' said Dr Jack.

CHAPTER XI

THE LEGITIMATE VISITORS

THEY reached the camp in safety, to find the girls once more moving about, busy with their preparations. It is true that Miss Stewart had her right arm bandaged from elbow to wrist, while Margia Stevens had developed a huge lump on one side of her jaw, and Ilonka Barkocz looked as though she had been trying conclusions with a whole hiveful of bees. In addition, the Princess, Evadne, Maria Marani, and Hilda Bhaer went about their duties in a most subdued way.

'There are the culprits,' said Jem, pointing them out, as the two Guiders and the two doctors crossed the meadow. 'Don't they look like whipped puppy-dogs?'

At this moment, Joey Bettany looked up from her task of sharing out fried wafers of potato, and gave an exclamation, before she dropped her spoon into the dish and came racing across the field to greet her brother-in-law vociferously. 'Jem! We've been having adventures galore! How are Madge and Davie? Is the Robin all right? Can Stacie sit up yet? When are the others coming?'

'One moment,' said the doctor, taking her by the shoulders and standing at arm's length from her, while he looked up and down and noted the soft tan on her face and the rounding of the once pale cheeks, which even a few days of life in the open in this health-giving atmosphere had given her. 'Yes; you look more like yourself,' he said. 'Madge will be pleased with you. Now, haven't you anything pretty to say to Jack?'

Jo turned with a grin to Dr Jack. 'I forgot you in the excitement of seeing Jem,' she confessed, as she shook hands. 'It seems such *years* since we left the Sonnalpe. But it's jolly having you here, Dr. Jack. Have you heard from Maynie lately?'

Jack Maynard smiled. 'Had a letter this week. Mollie is very fit and well. She had been staying with your beloved Carty, and her letter was full of the baby.'

'Is Carty disappointed that it's a girl?' asked Jo.

'I don't think so. Mollie says she's one beam of joy the whole time. By the way,' he added casually, 'they are going to call her "Josephine" after you. Carty said she was sorry she couldn't ask you to be god-mother——'

'Thank goodness she can't!' interrupted Jo in heartfelt accents. 'That *would* be the finishing touch. Me a godmother! Can you picture it? I should have to come over all prim and proper with a vengeance, then!'

Dr Jack looked at her curiously. 'You'll have to grow up some day, Joey,' he said.

'Not a day before I have to! I'll be like Jo March in *Little Women*, and "wear my hair in two tails till I'm twenty!" sooner than do that!' declared Jo fervently.

'Well, aren't you grateful to Carty for naming her firstborn after you?' demanded Jem, thinking it time to change the subject.

'Yes. What are they going to call her for short, though?'

'Mollie didn't say,' replied Mollie's brother.

By this time they had reached the camp, and the rest of the Guides gave them a hearty welcome, after which Elsie Carr, who had already had one fight with Evadne over it, produced the bugle and made some weird noises on it.

'What may that little ditty be?' inquired Dr Jem.

'It's meant for "Come to the cook-house door, boys!"' explained Evadne. '*Mittagessen* is ready.'

'I see. But before we have it, I should like to examine the casualties.—Miss Stewart, may I see your arm? Hornets can leave a pretty venomous poison behind, you know.'

'You'd better see to the children first,' said Miss Stewart. 'Lonny got badly caught. I put some lotion on, but she's terribly swollen.'

'What *I* want to know,' said Miss Wilson, 'is how on earth those hornets came to sting you at all. What were you doing to anger them? And who did it?'

Evadne promptly slipped behind tall Anne Seymour, and three other people made themselves as small as possible.

'They—came,' said Jo laconically. 'Luckily we heard 'em coming.'

'Elisaveta found them, I think,' said Miss Stewart, submitting to having the bandage unwound from her arm. 'At least, she and Evadne and Maria and Hilda came tearing across the meadow from the wood, shrieking at the tops of their voices. I guessed what had happened, and ordered all the girls and Rufus into the commissariat-tent at once. Luckily Jo was there to make Rufus obey, and the girls simply fled. Lonny tripped up, though, over Margia, and one or two of the vanguard caught her. Margia would have been all right, but she stayed to help me pull Lonny into the tent. Juliet and Grizel had the flaps ready and pulled them to at once. We fastened all the spaces with safety-pins, so that there wasn't room for one to get in. The girls held them until they were pinned.

I must say they behaved remarkably well. There was no panic, and they were promptly obedient.'

'A very good thing for them that they were,' said the doctor, as he finished with the Guider, and pulled Ilonka to him. 'Now let's have a look at you, Lonny. They certainly seem to have vented their wrath on you! Lucky we brought that lotion in case of need. I fancied you might get one or two wasp-stings, but I didn't bargain for anything like this.'

He was sponging Ilonka's face with the lotion as he spoke, and she was standing, trying not to cry out as the cleansing sponge passed over the stings. He finished her, and attended to Margia. Then he went to the lake to wash his hands, after handing the bottle over to the captain, who received it with due gratitude.

The full story only came out while they were having *Mittagessen*. As Miss Wilson said later, it was just what might have been expected! The four writhed at this, but were thankful to escape so lightly.

When they had got all the facts and they were disentangled from a good deal of totally irrelevant matter, the story ran thus:

The Princess and Maria had been gathering sticks in one part of the wood, and Hilda and Evadne had been a little way along another path, not very far from them. Some evil spirit moved Evadne to look up as she reached one tree, and there she had seen, hanging from a bough, a curious thing like a blown-out paper-bag. She had called Hilda's attention to it, and the pair had speculated as to what it was. Catching sight of Elisaveta and Maria through the trees, they had called to them to come and look. None of the four could imagine what it could be, though they knew it was not what it seemed. Finally, the Princess had been seized with the brilliant idea that they might get it down by throwing sticks at it. No sooner said than acted on! The four each hurled a stick at the 'paper-bag,' and Evadne's shot, being heavier and more direct than the others, brought it down. To the horror of the girls, a stream of black things poured forth from it, buzzing with an anger that was unmistakable. With a wild scream, Evadne shrieked 'Wasps!'—though why she should have imagined it was a wasps' nest no one ever found out. Still, the word was enough for the others. They took to their heels and fled back to camp, shrieking like lunatics the whole way. The rest of the story has been told. They had stayed in the tent, afraid to leave it until the hum of the furious hornets suddenly ceased, when Miss Stewart, greatly daring, opened a flap and peered out. Finding that the enemy had evidently gone, presumably to attack some other foe, she had let them all out.

'I only hope they don't hurt anyone very badly,' Miss Stewart concluded.

'They'll hurt no one any more,' said Dr Jack, making a long arm for some plums. 'They're all dead.'

Then the two doctors, with the aid of the captain and Miss Nalder, had to tell their part of the tale, and before it was finished the sound of voices and laughter through the trees told them that their other guests were at hand. And *Mittagessen* was not over!

'Never mind,' said Joey comfortingly. 'Think what a lot of news we have for them! *They* won't worry!'

Nor did they. By the time welcomes had been lavished on them and they had heard of the hornet raid, of the result of Juliet's fishing, of Jo's accident and her remarks to the captain, to say nothing of the midnight burglar on the first night, they were mopping their streaming eyes and holding their sides. Jo's affair particularly took their fancy. Madge laughed till she could laugh no more. Gisela said, with a sigh, 'It seems that you will never grow up, my Jo!'

'I should think not,' said Jo. 'Own up, Gisela! You wish you could be in it all! Don't you?'

Gisela shook her head doubtfully. 'I wonder. I should not like to fall into a pit, nor to fish up a dead body which turned out to be a lay-figure——'

'Mean!' cried Juliet, laughing. 'Well, those Poppies seem to have finished washing-up, and it's too hot for drill or anything like that. Shall we go round the camp?'

Mrs Russell agreed, and the visitors were escorted all round the camp and shown everything of interest. When that was over, since the heat still persisted, they retired to the shelter of the forest and rested until it was time for *Kaffee und Kuchen*. After that, they had a short sing-song, and then the five visitors were obliged to set off for home.

Wanda, whose small son was only two months old, was especially anxious to get back. It was the first time she had left him for so long; but her mother, Frau von Eschenau, was at the Sonnalpe, and had volunteered to take charge of him and his welfare, so that his young mother might take this chance of seeing the camp. 'We go to Salzburg almost at once, you know, Joey,' she said wistfully to Jo, as they walked together to the waiting cars. 'Friedel had a good position there, and we have a lovely little house on the Mönchsberg. You must come and visit us at Christmas. There are winter sports then, and Salzburg is so gay. You would enjoy it, I know.'

'I should love it—*after* Christmas,' said Jo. 'But I want to be with my own folk for then. But if Madge says I may, and you still want me, Wanda, I'll come for the New Year like a shot.'

'Then that is settled,' agreed Wanda. 'Marie will be with me, for it is so much nearer to school for her than Wien that mamma has decided that all the remainder of her holidays while she is at school must be spent there.'

'That is only two more,' said Marie herself, with a sigh. 'One grows up so soon!'

'But growing up has its compensations,' said her sister consolingly.

'Can't think of any!' growled Jo.

Wanda smiled to herself. 'You will—later. Here's the car. Good-bye, Jo, and do try not to be rude to any of the Guiders during the rest of the camp, will you not?'

Jo looked at her helplessly. 'If only the whole crowd weren't here, I'd show you what I thought of you for that, Wanda von Eschenau——'

'Wanda von *Glück*, if you please,' laughed Wanda. 'What would Friedel say, Joey?'

'Are you coming next Saturday?' asked Joey, ignoring this.

'I fear not. We—Friedel and little Kurt and I—hope to be in Salzburg by then. But I will write.'

'What is that?' demanded Madge, as she reached them. 'Jo, I have a message for you from the Robin. I forgot to give it to you before. She sends her best love, and she's written a fairy story.'

'Oh, good!' cried Joey. 'Give her my love, and tell her I'm longing to see it. Are you bringing her next week, Madge?'

Mrs. Russell shook her head. 'That is more than I can say, Joey. It depends on how she is, how the weather is, and whether I can come. I'm rather tied these days, you know, what with Robin and David and the twins, to say nothing of Stacie. Take care of yourself, little girl! And keep an eye on Elisaveta.' She bent to kiss her sister as she spoke, before pulling on her driving-gloves.

Joey returned the kiss and stood back. The others crowded up, and the head-girl was seized on by her brother-in-law.

'Good-bye Jo. You are looking twice as fit as when you left the Sonnalpe. If we can manage it, some of us will be over next Saturday. Mind you keep whole till then. I understand the nearest doctor here is seven leagues distant.'

'Righto!' said Jo. 'Good-bye, Jem.' She turned to Jack Maynard. 'Good-bye. Dr Jack; when you write to Maynie, give her my love, and say I'm furious she didn't come for a holiday.'

'You'd better write yourself,' replied Dr Jack, looking at her with a funny expression.

Jo caught it. 'What's happening to her?' she asked.

'We-ell—I suppose you've got to know sooner or later. Her husband has got a berth in New Zealand, and they're sailing almost immediately.'

Stunned, Joey let her hand drop, and he took advantage of it and got into the car. They were off before she had recovered from the sudden shock, and the others were crowding round, asking what was wrong with her.

'Have you heard the latest?' demanded Jo, glaring round at them all. 'Maynie is going to New Zealand to live—Dr Jack has just told me. She's going at once, and *she's not coming to say good-bye!*'

CHAPTER XII

JOEY'S LEG IS PULLED, WITH UNEXPECTED RESULTS

THE noise the Guides made when they heard the latest news of Miss Maynard, once favourite mistress in the school, now Mrs Alastair Macdonald, outdid anything they had accomplished at the Baumersee so far. Except Violet Allison, Ruth Wynyard, Lilli van Huysen, and Greta Macdonald—no relation!—all of them had been her pupils, and all of them had loved her dearly. To think that she could go to the other side of the world without so much as coming to see them—'Even for *one* day!' as Simone said—seemed unheard of to them.

'But—not coming to bid us farewell?' cried Frieda.

'Not a farewell to anyone,' replied Jo. 'Dr Jack says they are sailing almost at once.'

'But—not to see Madame and David, even?' asked Marie, her lovely face flushing.

'Apparently not.'

"Well, I think Maynie's real *mean*!' proclaimed Cornelia.

'Why ever couldn't her wretched husband get a job in England or Scotland?' demanded Grizel. 'New Zealand? Why, we shall never see her again!'

'Oh, it's not so bad as all that,' said Miss Wilson drily. 'Even if it were, there are such things as letters. You don't imagine that she will forget everyone here the moment she leaves England?'

'But New Zealand!' said Simone, with an indescribable gesture.

'Well, it's quite a civilised country,' said Miss Stewart, who had brothers out there. 'Don't look so doleful, girls! She is almost certain to come back to England for visits to her people, and then she will come to us. I shouldn't be in the least surprised if she broke her journey to come here. She always said that the years she was at Briesau were among the happiest in her life.'

'I can't think why she ever married,' grumbled the Princess. 'It's all very well for those who live about the Tiernsee, like Joey and Grizel and Juliet. Even the people who live in Innsbruck will have a chance of seeing her. But what about us who don't. She won't bother to come to Belsornia. And Vanna and Giovanna live in Italy, and Simone in Paris, and Paula and Lonny in Hungary, and lots of you in Wien. How could she rush round the Continent visiting everyone?'

'The only thing to do will be for everyone who can manage it to come to Briesau for a trip,' said the captain. 'There are plenty of hotels. Those who cannot stay at the school can go to them.'

'Yes; and there's sure to be some tiresome state thing, so that *I* can't come!' growled Elisaveta, who was by no means prepared to look on the bright side.

'Oh, Maynie will manage somehow,' said Jo cheerfully. 'Don't be so gloomy, 'Veta. Anyone would think she was dead, to hear you.'

'She might just as well be, for all the good she'll be to us at the other side of the world,' said Grizel mournfully, as they reached camp again.

'No, she mightn't cried Juliet. 'She *will* write. She couldn't do *that* if she were dead.'

'I think you are all very silly children,' said the captain severely. 'It's getting dusk, now. Hurry up and get *Abendessen* ready. You'll feel better when you've had a meal.'

'That is what grown-ups always say,' murmured Frieda sceptically to Jo, as they went off to the commissariat-tent together.

Jo made no response. She had been rather stunned by the news. Miss Maynard had come to the Chalet School half-way through its first term, and she had seemed almost like one of the foundation-stones. That she should go off to New Zealand was almost unbelievable. That she could do so without coming first to say good-bye to them, really was.

It may have been the shock of the news, but it is certain that Elisaveta, Hilda, Evadne, and Giovanna heard nothing more about their latest exploit, so it proved to be an ill wind that blew *some*body good. *Abendessen* was prepared and eaten to the tune of continual wonder as to the actions of 'Maynie,' and they were still talking of it when the whistle went for 'Lights out.'

The next day, being Sunday, was spent very quietly. In the morning all those who wanted to go attended Mass in the little chapel in the village. The rest took it in turns to read the Epistle, Gospel, and Collect for the day among themselves, and afterwards separated to read quietly or see to *Mittagessen* till the others returned. In the afternoon they sought the shade as usual, and most of them slept, for the heat still continued. The evening was spent in listening to a reading by the captain from *The Little Flowers of Francis*, a favourite book at the Chalet, and then going for a stroll along the shores of the lake.

Monday was spent in the ordinary camp work, topped off by a Nature expedition through the forest later on, and in the evening they had swimming and diving races. Miss Wilson had ascertained that they would be safe from any trouble with the pike so long as they kept to their own shores, so she gave permission for this impromptu regatta willingly, and, with the other two Guiders, joined in the fun.

Tuesday was much the same, and so was Wednesday. But on Thursday, Juliet, who had had a long confab with Grizel the night before, and had been up before anyone else in the camp that morning, sat down beside Jo and her 'gang' at *Mittagessen*, and apparently quite casually, said in the course of conversation, 'By the way, Joey, ever been back to look at that pit of yours again?'

'Had no time,' said Joey. 'Why?'

'Well, I should have liked to explore it. The captain said it must be at least a hundred years old, judging by the amount of rubbish there. It was right in the heart of the woods, you know. I doubt if many people have seen it. You said you didn't think it was a natural pit——'

'No; I'm sure it wasn't,' interrupted Jo. 'It looked far more as though someone had dug it, and the rain and wind had rounded it off a bit before dead branches and leaves covered it over. O-o-oh! Wasn't I scared when I went in? I couldn't imagine what had happened.'

'You weren't as scared as Vanna,' laughed Marie. 'She vowed you had been swallowed up. I never saw anyone more horrified about anything.'

'But it must have been a very horrid feeling, to slip down and down, and not know where you were going,' added Simone.

'I was all right. I landed on a heap of leaves, so I wasn't much hurt. I didn't like it down there, though—it was so dark, and seemed so full of creepy-crawlies—though, as I never found one when I undressed, I suppose I must have imagined *them*,' replied Jo, as she sucked meditatively at a slice of melon.

Frieda leaned back for a basket, and offered it to her. 'Have another slice, Joey. You cannot possibly get anything more from that.'

'Thanks—I think I will!' And Jo helped herself to her fourth slice, and attacked it vigorously.

'You will be ill, my Jo,' said Simone. 'That is the fourth.'

'Fruit never makes me ill,' retorted Jo. 'It needs you for that!'

Simone, whose digestion was not her strongest point, subsided at this, and Joey enjoyed the rest of her fruit in peace.

'Well, what about making up a party to go and explore that hole of Jo's?' asked Grizel.

'Good idea! Bill won't mind; let's ask her.' And Jo turned round to where the captain sat at the next 'table,' chatting gaily to some of the junior Guides. 'Madame, may Juliet and Grizel and—and—all our crowd go this afternoon and explore that hole I fell into last week?'

Anyone watching the elder girls would have seen their faces fall at the mention of that very afternoon. Miss Wilson, however, shook her head. 'Not this afternoon, Joey. It's so hot, I want you people to stay quiet. This evening we are thinking of making up an expedition to climb the Gesslerhorn—that mountain over there. But you can go to-morrow if you like,' she added. 'Miss Stewart is going to finish the Boatswain's test for Elsie, Anne, and Louise; and I am taking most of the others to the farm to see the butter-making and the cheese, too. You folk have seen it all before in other farms, so if you like to cry off and go and explore your pit instead, you may, so long as you take ropes and flash-lamps with you.'

'Oh, thank you, Madame,' said Grizel, with a joyous smile which seemed out of all proportion to the boon granted. 'That's arranged, then, you people. We seven will go and have a look round Jo's pit. Who knows? We might find something worth having!'

'Buried treasure, do you mean?' asked Evadne eagerly. 'Oh, I think——'

But Grizel suppressed her promptly. 'What nonsense! Of course not—nor hornets' nests, either,' she added, greatly to the indignation of the four concerned with that affair. 'No; what I meant was that it's just possible that some soldier, say, home from the Napoleonic wars, may have dug the pit to hide his treasures—and *they* wouldn't be likely to be diamonds and rubies, as you obviously imagine, Evvy.'

Jo's eyes glowed at the words. 'Wouldn't it be wonderful if we did? Just think of it! We might even find some old despatch that Napoleon had written and that had been forgotten about—or never known!'

'You and your old Napoleon!' said Grizel scornfully. 'You're mad about him, Jo.'

'I doubt if we'll find anything like that, even,' put in Juliet, with a warning glance at Grizel. 'But we might find some old coins, or a medal, or something like that.'

'And what would a soldier of *Napoleon's* be doing, hiding his belongings up here?' demanded Margia. 'You all seem to forget what Jo is always rubbing into us, that Nap was the Tirol's enemy.'

'I'd forgotten that,' murmured Joey, crestfallen.

Miss Stewart laughed. 'I doubt if you find anything at all but sticks and dead leaves and pine-cones. But if you do, remember I want it for the museum.' For the Chalet School had decided to start a proper museum, the present affair being a very small one, contained in one cupboard with glass doors.

'You shall have whatever we get,' promised Jo.

'Unless it's anything of real value like a diamond ring,' laughed Marie; 'that, I'm afraid, we ought to advertise.'

'Oh, in that case, I'll waive my claim,' agreed Miss Stewart.

The topic dropped there; but anyone who was interested might have seen Juliet and Grizel steal off by themselves that afternoon and hide themselves in a crevice in the rocks far from the rest. There they remained until wild yells from Evadne, who had been sent to hunt them up, announced to them that *Kaffee* was ready, and more than ready. They came, but after *Kaffee* they vanished again, leaving the rest to see to the clearing up, and only returned in time to join the expedition up the Gesslerhorn.

Everyone went on this expedition, Rufus being left to guard the camp. Miss Wilson was satisfied by this time that they need fear nothing save a tramp, and it was unlikely that one should turn aside for the Baumersee. He would be much more likely to go straight on to the village. Still, she considered it best to be careful; so Rufus was left, after Jo had talked solemnly to him for a minute. The great, wise dog knew what was expected of him, and he set to work to pad slowly round the boundaries of the camp before he settled down in a place where he could keep vigilant watch over the tents.

The climb was a beautiful one, up the slopes of a grass-clad hill at first. Later, they passed through a belt of pine trees. Then they came out to the virgin rock, up which they toiled steadily till they reached the summit, from which they had a magnificent view of the surrounding country to the south and east. To the north and west higher mountains closed them in, some, even after such heat, crowned with white, as a mark of the eternal snows that lay there; others, with crests of trees. Beneath them gleamed the silvery waters of the Baumersee, with the white splashes marking their tents on the green of the meadow at the opposite side. Beyond, was the black mass of the pine-forest, with, here and there, blue feathers of smoke marking the scattered farms and huts of the inhabitants. To the south-east they could just see a faint, blue gleam.

Jo shouted with joy at the sight of it. 'That must be the

Tiernsee! See how blue it is! I had no idea we could see it from here.'

'Neither had I,' said the captain, as she shaded her eyes with her hand and looked in the direction in which Jo was pointing. 'I shouldn't have thought it possible.— Frieda! You know this district. Surely it is unusual to be able to see so far? Or are we nearer than I thought?'

'I don't know, Madame,' replied Frieda. 'I was here five years ago, when I was only a child. I don't remember anything about the distance.'

The three Guiders exchanged an amused smile at Frieda's words. To their minds, there was not such a big difference between twelve and nearly seventeen. Frieda was, to them, a child still. None of the girls saw it, which was as well. They were too busy looking at what Margia described as 'Our' lake, with a calm disregard for anyone else who might live on its shores.

'Well, it is a wonderful view,' said Miss Nalder at last, as she glanced at her watch. 'I could stand and look for hours. But—do any of you know the time? nearly twenty o'clock. What about *Abendessen*?'

'Oh, we shall come down faster than we came up,' said Jo airily.

'*Shall* we?' said Miss Wilson grimly. 'Have you forgotten that slippery grass slope? We shan't find *that* very easy to negotiate.— Come along, Guides! It has been a wonderful climb, and the view is well worth the trouble. But I don't want to be caught up here by nightfall. It will darken as we get farther down, remember, and we have to go through that wooded bit.'

'*I* shall get down that grass slope easily enough,' murmured Jo to her usual satellites, Marie, Simone, and Frieda. 'All the same, I suppose Bill is right, and we ought to go. That wood will be fairly dark to get through.'

They set off on the downward journey, and made good time over the rock. The wood *was* dusky, but they could still see.

'This is a really "dark and gloomy wood," isn't it?' said Jo, as she just avoided running into a sapling which had taken root in the middle of the path. 'Hurrah! We're nearly at the end of it—I can see daylight through the trees!'

'And now show us how you intend to do that slope easily,' demanded Marie. 'I don't see how anyone can. Just look at those children!' And she pointed at the Quartette, who were slipping and sliding as best they might down the slippery slopes.

'*I'll* show you,' returned Jo. They reached the top of the meadow-like land, and she sat down, tucking her skirts carefully round her. 'Give me a shove off, someone,' she said.

Still rather puzzled as to what she was about, Frieda did as she asked, and gave a vigorous push to her shoulders. Away went Jo, tobogganing over the short grass, now glassy with the continued heat. Peals of laughter from the rest followed her, and, with one accord, those Guides who were far enough away from the Guiders to get off without being called back, followed her example.

As soon as Miss Wilson saw what had happened—which was not at once, for she and Miss Nalder were behind to act as whippers-in to any straggler, and Miss Stewart was in front with the Quartette—she called out to put a stop to it. 'Girls—girls! I forbid you to do it! Joey—Frieda—Marie—all of you, stop and get on to your feet at once!'

She might as well have called to the wind. Once they were off, it was impossible for the girls to stop themselves on the slippery grass. They shot down to the bottom, where most of them rolled over and over, shrieking with laughter, while Miss Stewart, thoroughly startled when first Jo, then Frieda, then Maria and Simone tore past her, followed by several of the junior Guides, who had hailed with yells of joy this novel method of negotiating a difficult place, could do nothing but stand still, clutching at two of her escort, while forbidding the others to emulate naughty Jo and her friends.

They were well scolded when the captain reached them, and stood meekly at attention while she told them what she thought of them. But all the same, Jo felt that it was worth anything to have that glorious run, even though the ground had been bumpy in places, and she had torn a rent in her overall which she was condemned to sew the next morning.

Indeed, they were highly pleased with themselves, and found it hard to stop talking when 'Lights out' sounded. However, rules were rules, and the Guide Law ordains obedience, so they lay in silence—though Jo was chuckling to herself—when suddenly, on to the canvas there came a tremendous 'plop.' 'Rain!' she exclaimed, sitting up, as that first plop was followed by another and another. 'That's why we could see so far! What ninnies we were not to think of it!'

'We must loosen the guy-ropes,' said Marie, tumbling out of her blankets. 'Quick! Those junior Guides will never remember to do it, and if it is not done, then the ropes will tauten and snap, and the tents will come down on them!'

The three girls hurried into gum-boots and raincoats with sou'-westers to keep their heads dry. Then they picked up their electric torches, and, followed by Rufus, began to loosen their own guy-ropes.

'Goodness! How can they sleep through this?' muttered Jo, as she and Frieda left Marie struggling with the last, and made for the next tent.

'They are not. There is Simone with Anne and Louise at theirs. But I hope the others do. If they awake, Corney or Evvy is sure to touch the canvas just to see what really happens, and then it will let the water through.'

'Then we'd better not talk,' said Jo, as they reached one of the big tents where some of the juniors were.

Working swiftly, and, in the circumstances, silently, they loosened the ropes without arousing the inmates, and passed on to the next, the commissariat-tent. Marie had rejoined them, and the other three were hard at work on the tent occupied by Juliet and Grizel, who slept through the whole affair. Indeed, nearly everyone in camp did so. All were tired, and the long hours in the open air with plenty of wholesome food and rich milk were causing them all to sleep better than they had ever done before. At first, some of them had been prone to wakefulness, owing to the unusual sounds of night-time out-of-doors. But that was over now. Even 'Charlie' and Miss Nalder never awoke.

'Only Bill's to do now,' muttered Anne, as the six met in the open space near to the commandant's tent. 'There's six of us for it, so it won't take long.'

'Thank goodness!' said Jo vigorously. 'I never knew anything like the way these creatures sleep! The Seven Sleepers simply aren't in it with them!'

They reached the tent, and began their work with due caution for the sleeper within. Frieda was busy at a rope, and nearly had it loosened when a hand suddenly appeared under the side of the tent, and a startled voice asked, 'Who is that? What on earth are you girls doing?'

It was well that Frieda was not troubled with nerves. She did give utterance to a little gasp, but that was all.

Jo, who was next to her, answered for her. 'It's us, Madame. The rain's pouring down, so we thought we'd better see to the guy-ropes. Hope we didn't wake you?' she added doubtfully.

'You did! I couldn't think what had happened at first. Who are you? Jo—and Frieda? Who else? Come in, and tell me what you've done.'

They crowded into the tent and told her, and she nodded. 'Splendid! That was the right thing to do! Have you finished? Then get back to your own tents. Remember, if anyone is in the least damp, she is to change. You all have fresh pyjamas here?'

They all had, so she sent them off. Presently, when they were settling down, she appeared at the doors of the tents, with mugs strung on a strap in one hand and a large, steaming jug in the other. 'Hot milk,' she said. 'A mugful each all round to keep out any colds!'

'Not the Lady with the Lamp,' said Jo, as she accepted her share, 'but the Lady with the Jug! Thank you, Madame, it's delicious!'

After that, they snuggled down again, and nothing more was heard of any of them till the morning, when, once again, Juliet and Grizel were first up, and vanished off through the trees. They got back as quickly as possible, and Grizel, finding the bugle, blew 'Reveillé' as hard as she could.

'Come along!' called Juliet. 'Show a leg, there—show a leg!—Jo, get up, you lazy child!—Up, you three! It's a glorious morning, though it seems to have rained in the night. What on earth is the matter with you all?' as three peals of laughter greeted her last statement.

'Rained in the night! My dear, we were up and out in it, loosening the ropes!' explained Jo. 'How you *could* sleep through all the row the rain made on the canvas, I can't think! Must be the result of the way you all gorged at supper!'

'What's that?' asked Grizel, who had finished her tooting, hung up the bugle, and now came to join in the conversation.

'Joey's being rude—as usual,' said Juliet lightly, but with a funny little twinkle in her eyes. 'Come along, Grizel; we'd better see that the others are up.'

They strolled off, leaving a dumbfounded tent behind them.

'What has happened?' gasped Marie, who was the first to recover herself.

'I *said* it to make Juliet rise—and she hasn't risen!' cried Jo.

'Perhaps she saw it,' suggested Frieda, as she knelt to say her prayers.

'We had better hurry. The sun is shining, and it must be late.'

It *was* late, as they found when they were all dressed and scurrying about getting *Frühstück* ready. They had all slept in—except Juliet and Grizel, and they were silent about their early rising. Things were rather rushed that morning to get everything in, and Jo forgot the look she had seen on Juliet's face in answer to her rudeness. Consequently, when, the afternoon siesta over, 'Charlie' took her three would-be 'Boatswains' off to finish their test, and 'Bill' and Miss Nalder set out with their charges for the farm, the people who had begged off the latter expedition made their way through the wood, chattering amicably till they came to the pit, where they stopped, and looked down.

'It'll be awfully wet after all the rain that came down

through the night,' said Jo, as she gazed down into its depths.

'Not so very,' said Juliet, who was making a running-bowline at one end of the rope. 'It is sheltered by these trees, you see. And the tilt of the ground is away from it everywhere. It seems to have been dug in a little prominence.'

'Oh well, it can only make us muddy, and goodness knows there's always soap and water about,' said Jo, as slipped the noose over her shoulders. 'Anyone else coming down besides me?'

'Aren't we all going?' suggested Marie.

'We can't,' said Juliet with severe commonsense. '*Some*one must stay at the top to pull up those who go.— You said yourself, Jo, that it was impossible to climb out.'

'Very well. Then, two stay, and the rest of us will take it in turns to change with them,' said Joey. 'Who will stay first?'

'I will,' said Grizel quickly. 'Marie can stay with me, and later on someone can come up and relieve us.'

So it was arranged, and presently Jo, Juliet, Frieda, and Simone were all at the bottom of the pit, flashing their torches over the piled-up leaves and cones which carpeted the floor of it.

'No wonder you fell soft, Joey,' said Juliet. 'I should think it must be metres thick there!'

'But what do we do?' asked Frieda.

'Turn over the heaps and see if we find anything,' said Jo, whose imagination was beginning to soar. 'Do it carefully, so that you don't miss anything.'

They began, and found that Juliet had been right in saying that it would not be very wet. It was only the top layer which was damp. Beneath, it was quite dry. They worked for nearly half an hour, and Simone, who was a very matter-of-fact person, was just beginning to complain that it was a waste of time, when Jo suddenly uttered a queer sound, midway between a choke and a screech.

'Joey! What is it?' gasped Frieda.

'Is it tr-r-reasure, then, my Jo?' asked Simone, rolling her R's violently in her excitement.

'It's a packet!' panted Jo, who was pulling it out from under the leaves. 'See! It's done up in some oil-cloth kind of stuff! Oh!'

Frieda raised her voice. 'Grizel! Marie! Jo has found something! She's found something after all!'

'*No!* What is it?' demanded Grizel with flattering earnestness, as she hung over the pit. 'Shall we get the ropes and pull you up?'

'Not yet!' cried Joey. 'There may be more.—Dig where I found it, Simone!'

Simone and Frieda dug hard, but found nothing further, though they disturbed the rubbish of generations. Frieda returned to her own little corner and turned over the leaves there with eager fingers. Jo continued a little farther along. An hour passed, and Grizel was just about to lean over and call that she could hear voices from the camp, when a wild yell startled her and Marie. They leaned over again. Joey and Simone were dancing madly about, clutching another package.

'What on earth have you got there?' demanded Grizel, casting a startled glance at her fellow-conspirator.

'Another packet—fastened up in leather—a leather wallet!' cried Frieda.

'What on earth——' muttered Grizel.

Juliet shook her head. 'No idea at all. But it's more than time to go. Listen! There goes Bill's whistle!'

'Whistle, you people!' called Grizel. 'Look out! Here comes the rope!'

The four explorers were very reluctant to leave the pit, but they dared not disobey that whistle, so they climbed up with the aid of the rope and some tugging on the part of the two girls at the top. When they were up, they all tore down the paths till they reached camp, muddy, dirty, dusty, but triumphant.

'You don't mean to say you've found something?' exclaimed the captain, as she saw them.

'Two things—*two* things, Madame!' cried Frieda. 'Joey found one, and Simone the other.'

'No!' And the entire company surged round them, all thought of *Kaffee* gone.

They all squatted on the ground, and, with Scout knife and scissors, Jo and Simone opened their finds.

Jo's came first. She unrolled the strip of oil-cloth in which it had been tied up and disclosed to view—three brass buttons, a hastily-made clay plaque with what purported to be a bas-relief of Napoleon's head in profile on it, a red-spotted handkerchief, and a faded sheet of blue paper, on which something was written in German characters in very watery ink. Eagerly Jo spelled it out—Grizel was not very expert at German script—'Sold again!'

'Oh!' She cast it from her furiously. 'A rotten leg-pull!' she cried. 'Who was it—Juliet?—You, Grizel?'

What else she might have said no one will ever know, for at that moment, Simone had got her wallet open, and was emptying out its treasures. 'Jo!' she cried.

A faded blue ribbon, attached to a closed locket, the locket tarnished and with a curious brown stain across it; a packet of letters on yellowed paper that was very tender with age; a paper which, when opened, disclosed a tiny plait of flaxen hair, tied at either end with more faded blue ribbon; a rosary of black beads, the Crucifix as tarnished as the locket; a little prayer-book with the Office of the Mass in Latin. That was all, but the girls looked at them with awe and reverence, and all forgot the bogus packet which Juliet and Grizel had secreted in order to tease Jo.

The captain took the letters, opened, and glanced at them, and a curious tenderness came over her face. 'It is a true find, Guides,' she said, turning to them. 'Listen! These are the letters of a young Tirolean who was enrolled in the army of Andreas Hofer, and who fought against Napoleon. They are sent to him by his sweetheart, and he must have kept them about him always. His name was Gottlieb, in honour of the great Gottlieb Strönen, and hers was Mädel. They were to have been married the Christmas after he joined Hofer, and she writes lamenting that it cannot yet be. This letter tells how she is longing for him to return, and hopes that the wicked French will soon be driven out of their beloved country. This one bids him not to heed any stories he may hear of her having been ill, for there is nothing wrong with her but a cold which will go when the warm weather comes. *This* one'—and the captain's face saddened—'is in a different writing, and seems to be from a sister. It tells him that his Maädel has gone to the Blessed Paradise, where she promised, with her last breath, always to pray for him, and to wait at the Gates for him until he should come.' She opened a final scrap of paper. 'I will read this as it is written, girls—translating for those like Violet and Ruth who don't know much German yet. 'This letter came to me this morning, just at the dawn, brought by Andreas Hoffman. Two hours after I had it, I was shot through the chest. Our General saw, and bade them bear me hence. But when we had reached the Black Pinewood, I bade them set me down and return, for the French Usurper is strong, and needs must all our men give him battle. So I have crawled here, and will leave these things in the pit Mädel and I dug as children with her brother Friedrich, now in Paradise by the gateway of a soldier's death. Then I must try to get farther into the wood lest the enemy find me, and seek to learn our General's secrets from me. I . . ." It trails off there, girls,' went on Miss Wilson, 'as if the writer's strength had failed him. I do not know, of course, but I think he found escape—by way of the Gates of Paradise where his Mädel waited for him.'

She opened the locket, and there was the crude painting of a red-cheeked girl with flaxen plaits and blue eyes, attired in the Tirolean national bodice. She showed it to them, and then closed it, and laid it and the letters and rosary back into the wallet.

Nothing more was said about the joke. The girls were all busy thinking over this little faded love story of more than a hundred years ago. Very quietly they sat down to their *Kaffee*, and what chattering was done was done by the juniors.

Only when bed-time came, and the Cadets were standing with the Guiders at the flagstaffs, Joey spoke. 'Miss Stewart, we can't put *that* in the museum,' she said.

Miss Stewart nodded. 'I agree, Joey. The captain is going to try to find out if there are any descendants of theirs hereabouts who would like to have these relics. If not, they will be given to the priest, and he will do with them what he thinks best.'

For the sake of those who may be interested, it may be mentioned that a great-great-great nephew of Gottlieb was found in the big village seven leagues away, and he received this relic of his hero ancestor with deep gratitude. He and his cherish the old wallet and its pitiful contents as a very great treasure indeed. So the practical joke planned by Juliet and Grizel brought about a most unexpected result.

CHAPTER XIII

LAUNDERING DE LUXE

PERHAPS the discovery made in what the girls, with one accord, named 'Joey's Pit' had something to do with it. Perhaps they were settling down more soberly after the first wild adventures. The fact remains that the last week of their camping was much quieter than the first had been.

'A good thing, too,' said the captain when she was discussing it with the other two Guiders. 'Many more incidents such as we have had would have seen me with white hair before we got back to the Tiernsee.'

'Poor old thing!' laughed Miss Stewart. 'And the amazing part is,' she went on thoughtfully, 'that, except for the hornet business, everything has happened with the seniors.'

'Not quite everything,' put in Miss Nalder. 'You could scarcely say that the arrival of the midnight marauder was the fault of any of the girls. That was Rufus's affair entirely.'

'Well, Rufus is Jo's dog.'

'Still, she is scarcely to blame because he smells out

a thief. I think it was a very good thing he did so.'

'Oh, so do I. We should probably have lost a quantity of food—to say nothing of the danger of his returning another night with a few pals!'

The Guiders laughed again at this picture, and the subject dropped. Still, as Miss Stewart had pointed out, the middles had been remarkably free from evil-doing—for them. It was unique in their history, and not likely to happen again.

It may have been the reason for what did happen next, although it was certainly no evil-doing on their part, rather a desire to be truly helpful. Owing to sundry accidents they were running rather short of linen of all kinds. Most people were reduced to their last overalls, and handkerchiefs were at a premium. In an evil moment, Elsie Carr, Margia Stevens, Evadne Lannis, Cornelia Flower, and Ilonka Barkocz began to discuss it.

'I'm down to my last hankey,' said Margia, regarding, with an air of disapproval, the soiled rag she had taken from her pocket.

'So am I,' said Ilonka, producing one which might have been a shade better than her friend's but was certainly no more.

'My overall is the limit,' sighed Elsie. 'It's never recovered from that slip I had the night it poured so after Gottlieb's things were found in Jo's Pit. It really is disgraceful. If Bill didn't know it was the last I have, she'd say things!'

'*All* my lanyards are filthy,' observed Cornelia. 'Hello,' she added in a different tone of voice, 'here's Veta and Paula and Cyrilla. My goodness me! What *have* they been doing?'

She might well ask. All three were dripping wet and covered with green weed from head to foot. The Quartette —which on occasions became a Quintette when Ilonka was about—rose to their feet, and, keeping their three friends at a safe distance, demanded, 'What on earth have you three been up to?'

'It was 'Veta's fault,' said Paula. 'She fell into the pond at the farm, and Cyrilla and I tried to pull her out——'

'And were so clumsy, they fell in themselves,' added Elisaveta calmly.

'Well, I should advise a bath,' said Elsie, keeping well to the windward of the three. 'It's to be hoped you've none of you swallowed any of the stuff, for, judging by the smell, I should think it was rank poison—full of germs and things.'

' 'Veta *must* have, 'cos her mouth was open when she fell in,' said Syrilla.

'Then go and get your things off, and bathe at once,' said Elsie firmly. 'I'll make you a hot drink of some kind, and you'd better take a dose of something in case of accidents. I know where Bill has the key of the medicine-chest. I'll get it, and see what there is.'

Accordingly, when the three came up out of the lake, clean once more, they were greeted with a jorum each of something that smelt rather worse than the pond-weed had done, and looked horrible.

'What's that?' demanded the Princess.

'Medicine—to keep you three from having typhoid fever,' said Elsie.

'No, thanks! I'd rather not be poisoned, if it's all the same to you,' retorted the Princess decisively.

But she was not to escape.

'Poison? It's no such thing,' cried Evadne indignantly. 'It's just a good dose of something—er—two or *three* things—to keep you from getting ill.'

The three protested vigorously, but it availed them nothing. Finally, Cornelia clinched the argument by saying, 'Well, if you won't think of anything else, think of Madame—I mean *our* Madame, not Bill! In a way, she's responsible for us.'

' 'Specially 'Veta,' added Evadne. 'You *are* a tremendous responsibility, you know, 'Veta, old thing.'

'Yes,'—Elsie was quick to seize her chance—'if anything happens to you, your government would say it was *her* fault. They might even drag her to Belsornia to stand her trial,' she added cheerfully.

Elisaveta had no idea as to whether this was likely or not; but she adored Mrs Russell, so, very reluctantly,

113

she agreed to drink the mixture, provided she was told what was in it.

'After you've taken it—not before,' said Elsie. 'I give you my word of honour, though—*Guide* honour—that it's none of it poison—or castor-oil,' she added, remembering that the Princess had an invincible dislike for this time-honoured remedy.

'Oh—well! I suppose it's all right,' said Elisaveta; and drank with both eyes shut. As the last drop went down, she opened them, flinging away the mug with a wild shudder. 'Ur-r-r-rh! Whatever on earth was it? Of all the horrid things I've ever tasted, that was the worst!'

'It makes me feel sick!' wailed Cyrilla.

'Sick? I'm poisoned!' declared Paula, pulling fearful grimaces. 'Own up, you three! What *was* it?'

'It was all good, anyhow,' said Elsie. 'There was syrup of figs, Gregory powder, liquorice powder——'

'And Bill had some senna pods standing in a glass—she was mixing them for Hilda because she's been head-achey, and 'fessed that she'd eaten half a pound of chocolate in the night because she felt so hungry,' put in Cornelia. 'I just tipped the liquid into your mugs, and set some more for Hilda.'

'And it's a blessing those mugs were enamel and not pot,' added Evadne. 'The way you chucked them down . . .' Words failed her.

The martyred three stood stock-still, and glared at the Quintette in silence, which was broken by Ilonka. 'Won't you catch cold?' she asked in a detached voice. 'I think you ought to dress.'

'Dress!' burst from the Princess.

'Yes; dress,' said Elsie. 'You know—get some clothes on, and hang those swimming-suits of yours out to dry.'

The awful truth broke from Paula first, though the other two were not far behind. 'I cannot dress. I have used all my clothes,' she announced.

'Used all your clothes? What *do* you mean?' inquired Evadne.

'I brought only three changes, and this was the last.'

'And that was *my* last!' wailed Elisaveta.

'I also,' added Cyrilla. Then an awful thought struck

114

her. 'Must we stay in bed until they send us fresh clothes from home?'

Now the Quintette were in the camp, firstly to look after it—with the aid of Rufus—secondly to have *Kaffee und Kuchen* ready for the rest when they should return from a ramble. Grizel had been left nominally in charge, but she had been kept awake all the previous night with earache, and, before the party had gone off, Miss Wilson had given her something to ease the pain and advised her to lie down for a while. The girls left in charge were old enough to be trusted—Elsie and Evadne were fifteen, and Ilonka was nearly sixteen—and they had all been so much steadier during the last few days, she thought no harm could come of their being left for an hour or two to look after themselves. Unfortunately, Elisaveta, Cyrilla, and Paula had fallen into the pond and disposed of their last change of clothes. It was obvious that *some*thing must be done about it.

'If it had been the first week instead of half-way through the second,' said Elsie, 'some of us could have lent you what you need. As it is, we're all down to our last batch of clothes.'

'Guess they'll just have to sort out the best of what they've worn before, and wear them,' said Evadne.

'None of mine are fit to wear,' said the Princess sadly. 'I don't know how it is, but I just seem to *attract* thorns and briars and dirt. Bill said rude things about the last lot she saw.'

Then it was that Ilonka was seized with her brilliant idea. 'Of course, we must wash them,' she said.

The rest patted her on the back as soon as they had recovered from the shock this simple suggestion gave them. It was a brainwave. They would do not only sets of clothes for the distressful three, but oddments for *every*one! They would have a clear two hours in which to perform. Grizel was not likely to disturb them, and the weather was hot again, and the things would dry very quickly.

Sending the forlorn trio to wrap themselves in blankets and bring the least soiled of their garments, the Quintette set to work at once. Elsie set the dixies on the fire, while

Ilonka filled them with water, and Evadne fed the flames. Cornelia dashed off to the commissariat-tent in search of soap, and returned with two tablets of cold-tar toilet soap—all she could find. Margia found a knife, and began to cut one tablet into tiny pieces, which she put into one of the buckets. On this they poured hot water as soon as the first dixie was ready, soap frothed up. 'It's important to have a good lather,' said Elsie in professional tones.

When this was ready, they dumped into it a miscellaneous assortment of garments, paying no heed to what was coloured and what was white. Guide overalls, handkerchiefs, underclothes—all went in together! The other three, wrapped in blankets, and looking not unlike Indian squaws, sat in the door of the nearest tent, and gave advice.

'I've seen the women at home washing in the rivers,' said Elisaveta. 'They put the things on one stone and bang them with another.'

'Well, we're not going to do that, anyhow,' said Elsie stirring her washing with the stick. 'Get some cold water, Evvy, and then we can put our hands in and rub.'

Evadne and Ilonka brought up two buckets of cold water and they managed to get some poured in. Then the five washer-women each selected a garment, rubbed soap on it, and set to work to rubbing with a vim that would have finished anything less durable than a Guide overall.

'I say,' said Margie after a moment or two, 'I don't believe we should have put everything in like that. The colour's coming out of those overalls and the white things are looking all streaky.'

With a yell, Elsie, who had constituted herself head washer-woman, dashed at the bucketful, and dragged out what was left in with more speed than care. As a result, she tipped the lot on to the grass, and a few pleasing stains of green were added to the white things before they were all picked up. Luckily, most of the soap was setting in a thick lather at the bottom, and they did not lose much of it. Another bucket was brought, and into it were put the white things, looking sadly streaked and stained. The girls set to work on the overalls again, and presently

Cornelia ran down to the lake with hers and rinsed it out. Then she brought it back. 'It's wet,' she said.

'I know how to wring, anyhow,' said Elsie. 'I've got a post-card at home of two Scottish washer-women, and they each take an end and twist different ways so that the water is all squeezed out.—Come along, Corney. You keep that end, and I'll take this.'

In less than three minutes that overall had been twisted and wrung till the wonder was that there was any moisture left in it at all—or that all the threads were not broken. Finally, they untwisted it and shook it out. It looked queer, and not at all like the freshly-laundered overalls to which they were accustomed. Still, as Cornelia argued, it *must* be clean—it had been so thoroughly rubbed and rinsed and wrung. They hung it up on a bush to dry, and went on to the next. At length, nine overalls were hanging on the bushes, and if they looked queer and patchy, still, it was certain they were clean, and that was the main thing.

The white things were much more trouble. Evadne had an idea that you boiled white things. But when they had tried, and let two or three handkerchiefs burn to the bottom of a pan, they decided to give up and rely on rubbing only.

'Ought not they to be starched?' inquired Paula, with her head on one side.

'I dare say,' said Elsie shortly. 'There isn't any starch.'

'Oh, but you can make it of corn-flour!' cried Evadne eagerly. 'I know Jeanne starches Momma's laces that way.'

'Sure?' asked Elsie doubtfully.

'Certain!'

'Very well.—Margia, do go, like a lamb, and see if you can find some in the commy-tent.'

Margia went off, and presently returned with a yellow packet. 'This do?' she asked.

'Fine,' said Elsie. 'Now then, Evvy, as you know so much about it, you'd better make the starch.'

Evadne had watched her mother's maid often enough to know what to do. The thing she did *not* know was the correct quantity. However, she was not going to own to this before Elsie. So she trusted to luck; decided that she might as well mix a good supply while she *was* about it and emptied the whole of the packet into the bowl Cornelia had brought her. She mixed the starch to a paste, and then added the hot water, till she had it about the consistency of creamy milk. Then she sat back. 'There now,' she said. 'Dip the things into that, and leave them a minute or two, and then all you have to do is take them out.'

'Wring them?' asked Elisaveta, who was interested in all this.

'N-n-no; I don't think so. Jeanne just pats the laces in a cloth.'

'We'd need a sheet for some of these things!' protested Margia.

'Well, I believe that when she does bigger things, she rolls them up and leaves them for a bit.'

'I see. Well, we'll pat the hankies and so on, and the other things we'll just roll up. I expect that's all right. It *sounds* all right.' and Elsie suited the action to the word.

They worked hard, and by the time Grizel, refreshed and fit after her long quiet sleep, had roused up, everything was done, and their implements were put away, so that she had no idea what they had been doing. It is true that she raised her brows when she saw the overalls Elisaveta, Paula, and Cyrilla were wearing; but she said nothing, beyond asking if they had been to bed in them. The trio said, 'No, Grizel!' and opened innocent eyes at her. They were not exactly comfortable—wearing roughly dried clothes is *not* comfortable as a rule. But they felt clean, and that was the main thing. The rest of the affair came out later, when the others arrived home, tired and hungry after a long tramp, and demanded *Kaffee und Kuchen* as soon as possible. It was ready, for the washer-women had refused to let the other three help with the washing, but had ordered them, so soon as they were dressed, to get the meal ready.

'Hasn't this stuff got a queer taste?' said Jo, as she set down her mug of coffee.

'Yes—soapy,' replied Simone. 'Who made it?'

'Us,' said Elisaveta. 'We—er—helped get it ready.'

'Then what on earth have you put in it?' demanded

118

Anne Seymour from the next table. 'It tastes like a wash-ing-day.'

The eight looked at each other. They had forgotten to rinse out the dixies which had been pressed into service for the washing, and there was no doubt about it—the coffee was redolent of coal-tar and tasted strongly of soap.

'What have you been doing?' asked Juliet, catching their furtive glances. 'Grizel, what wickedness have these people been doing?'

'They were very good,' said Grizel indignantly. 'I never even heard 'Veta and Paula and Cyrilla come back. I was amazed when I saw them.'

'You would have been more amazed if you had seen them then,' said Frieda, laughing. 'They fell into that terrible pond over there, and it is stagnant, as you know. They were one mass of weeds, and the smell was horrible!'

'That reminds me,' called the captain from the farthest table. 'I want you three to have some medicine to-night, to carry off the effect of your bath.'

The thought of having to take more medicine finished the trio's caution.

'Madame, we've taken some!' cried Paula. 'It was terrible! Do say we need take no more!'

'Taken some?' exclaimed Miss Wilson. 'But where did you get it? Who gave it to you?'

'I did,' said Elsie, getting to her feet.

'You?' There was a moment's pause. Then the captain said curtly, 'Explain, please!'

Elsie explained—helped out by the rest of her clan. 'When we saw the awful stuff they were covered with and must have swallowed, we thought they might get——'

'Typhoid fever,' put in Margia. 'So we dosed them with——'

'Guess the horridest mixture of the lot!' Thus, Evadne. 'Elsie got the key of the medicine-chest, and took some liquorice powder and Gregory——'

'And I—I took the syrup of figs,' added Ilonka.

'And I saw the senna you'd mixed for Hilda, so I added it to the lot, and put some more to soak,' contributed

119

Cornelia. 'Then we stirred it all up, and made three lots of it, and they drank it——'

She got no further. The Guiders had been listening to the rigmarole with faces over which the most varying expressions chased each other. They dared not look at each other, but, just as Cornelia got to the end of her remark, Miss Stewart inadvertently caught Miss Nalder's eye, and they both went off into shrieks of laughter, in which Miss Wilson joined. The eight glared at them. They could see nothing funny in the matter.

Margia spluttered. 'Yes; an' then we went an' washed their clothes—and things for some of you others—an' all you can do is to laugh!' she cried.

'Bill's' laughter ceased on the spot. 'You *what*?' she exclaimed.

'Washed their clothes,' said Elsie.

'But none of you have your Laundress badge!'

'Well, we did the best we could,' said Evadne sulkily.

'Let me see the clothes.'

The trio got up and marched round, and Miss Wilson examined the streaky overalls in dead silence. They had been left in the full glare of the sun, to dry them quickly, and they were faded in patches. This combined with the effects of the 'washing,' had made them the most unsightly garments imaginable.

'What else did you wash?' asked the captain at length.

They told her, enumerating the various garments. Finally, Elsie, feeling that it was as well that everything should come out at once, added, 'And we starched them —with corn-flour starch.'

Miss Wilson got up from the groundsheet. 'Where are they?' she demanded.

'Over there, on the shore. We thought we'd better bleach them, as the colour from the overalls had run and they were a bit stained. So we spread them out, and they were drying nicely the last time we looked,' said Margia.

With one accord the entire company went to see what had happened. The Guiders were first; the rest came close behind.

Among other things, the would-be laundresses had washed about twenty handkerchiefs, three camisoles, and a pillow-case belonging to Miss Stewart, who possessed one of those skins which cannot suffer wool in any shape or form next to them. She said afterwards that she was only thankful they had not been inspired to try to wash a sheet for her!

Not being very sure what white things should be starched, they had decided to risk it, and starch the lot. The captain picked up a handkerchief, and cried out in dismay as she felt it like a piece of board. The others were the same. The camisoles were no better, and as for the pillow-case, it was stuck firmly together.

'I believe,' said Miss Nalder in a shaky voice, 'that these things would literally stand by themselves.'

It was the only comment passed at the moment, though 'Bill' found plenty to say later on. The washer-women sadly picked up the results of their activities and carried them solemnly to the lake, where the captain instructed them to soak the maltreated articles till the starch was out of them once more. Later, she called them together, and forbade them to touch the medicine-chest; to dose each other; and to wash garments until they had their Laundress badge. 'If you had waited,' she concluded, 'you would have found out that to-morrow we are having a real washing-day, and you would have learned something about it. As it is, you have simply put us all to a great deal of trouble. And you might have poisoned those three!'

They were very subdued about it, but secretly they all agreed with 'Charlie' when she announced firmly, 'Well, whatever else happens, one thing is sure: every Guide in the Chalet School who has not yet gained her Laundress is going to take that Test next term, or my name isn't Constance Elizabeth Stewart!'

'At any rate, we've got her Christian name out of it,' said Margia that night just before 'Lights out.' 'I've always wanted to know what it was, and we've never been able to find out, as everything is just marked "C. E. Stewart." It might have been worse!'

CHAPTER XIV

THE WIND-UP OF CAMP

"THE last day!' sighed Joey on the Monday morning following the washing-day of the Quintette. 'Oh, how sorry I am!'

'I also,' agreed Frieda, coming up behind her. 'It has been a splendid holiday.'

'It's been an eventful one,' said Juliet, who was with Jo. 'Well, all good things come to an end.'

'Oh, don't be trite!' groaned Jo. 'I loathe popular sayings!'

'Can't help it. It happens to be true. Never mind. If it *is* the last day, it's obviously going to be a fine one. We have really been very fortunate with the weather. When it's rained, it's rained in the night; and the days have been so hot that the damp has dried up almost immediately.'

"We've got our Boatswain's badge, anyway,' said Elsie with satisfaction. 'I only want one more to make my First-class Guide badge possible. I didn't think I'd be able to get it next term. But if I work at Laundress—and I'm going to do *that* all right—I shall.'

'By the way, have you heard the latest about school?' asked Jo, turning from the lake and facing the little crowd that stood about.

'That depends on what it is,' said Simone. 'What is it, my Jo?'

'I wish you'd drop that silly trick of "my" Jo as though I belong to you and no one else,' grumbled Jo. Then, seeing that Simone looked pink and tearful, she went on. 'This is something quite fresh. Bill and the others were so horrified over the washing of the Quintette, that they've decided to suggest to Mademoiselle and my sister that a Domestic Economy side should be added to the school, and every girl is to have at least two terms in it.'

'But, Domestic Economy—what is that?' asked Marie.

'Oh, cooking, and washing, and housework, and so on,' said Juliet. 'It's a very good idea.'

'I think so, too,' said Frieda. 'If we should wed, and have learned housewifery at school as well as what we learn at home, we shall be able to make happy homes for our husbands and children.'

'More than that,' added Miss Wilson, who had joined them in time to hear Frieda's last sentence. 'Every woman, whether she be peasant or princess, should know how to keep house. It should be a part of every girl's education. I dislike the habit so many English schools have of turning out girls who can construe Horace, but are unable to cook a dinner; who can work out a theorem in Geometry, but cannot patch a shirt; who can read French and German in the original, or know all about the growth of Parliament, or the course of the Trade Winds, and yet who cannot wash a pair of socks or bath a baby.'

'But we do that in Child Nurse!' protested Marie.

'I know,' replied Miss Wilson. 'But not every school runs Guides. In many schools where Companies may be found, there are yet girls who are non-Guides. Now this is all wrong. Eve's first work when she left the Garden of Eden was to be a homemaker. Of that, I am sure. It should be our first work, too. I know that many people talk a lot of nonsense about women being emancipated from such "drudgery." Believe me, girls, the woman who is above tending her husband and children or—if God does not give her those—helping other women who need such help, is a poor creature, developed on one side only. And we are not meant to be that. We are sent into the world to develop as many sides of us as possible. What would you think of a rose that produced petals on one side only? You would say that it was deformed. And woman, when she tries to ignore the human side of life, is deliberately deforming her nature.'

'But there are some women who never can learn homey sort of things, aren't there?' asked Jo doubtfully.

'That is true, Joey. But they are in the minority—very

123

much in the minority. And none of you can plead that lack.'

'Oh, but I don't want to!' exclaimed Elsie. 'I think it will be jolly fun.'

'I am very glad to hear it,' said 'Bill.' Then she smiled suddenly. 'It won't begin next term, though, girls. We must discuss it very thoroughly, and see how we are going to manage. At soonest, we shall not begin till after Christmas. Do you realise that school is not quite a fortnight off?'

'Goodness!' cried Jo. 'I'd forgotten it was so near!'

'And I've got to go back to Belsornia and be proper again,' sighed the Princess. 'I only wish I need not.'

'Never mind,' said Jo. 'We've still got to-day, and we'll make a glorious day of it for a good wind-up.'

'What shall we do?' asked Frieda.

'Suppose you all come back to camp,' said Miss Wilson. 'We'll hold a meeting, and see what we can suggest.'

They followed her back to camp, where the people still on fatigues were busy. She blew her whistle, and they all stopped what they were doing and turned expectant faces in her direction.

'Listen, Guides!' she called. "Hurry with your work, and finish. We are going to have a meeting to decide how we shall spend the last day.'

There was a cheer, and the Guides returned to their duties, working with a vim that in one or two cases seemed likely to lead to disaster. Cornelia, peeling potatoes, nearly gave herself a nasty cut; and Vanna, counting out sausages, which were to form the chief dish at *Mittagessen,* upset the lot, and Rufus, who was standing by, contrived to wolf two down before Jo could stop him. 'You wicked thief!' she cried, cuffing him soundly. 'You *know* that's not permitted! Go to the tent!'

With head and tail down, Rufus trotted off dejected to the tent, there to collapse in a heap, and lie waiting the joyful moment when his mistress would come and forgive him.

Meanwhile, the Guides had finished their work and were collecting about the mound between the flag-staffs, where the Guiders were seated. When they were all there, the captain called for silence, and then asked for suggestions as to what they should do on that last day. 'And one at a time please,' she added. 'Remember that, whatever you choose, we must pack up as far as possible this evening, leaving only our paliasses to dismantle, and the tents to strike to-morrow. The charabancs will be on the road for us at ten o'clock, and we don't want too big a rush at the last. So be reasonable, girls, I implore you.'

They chattered, as Miss Nalder said like a rooks' parliament; but at length, they decided that they would do nothing special.

'Just do our ordinary camp duties, and have our meals at the usual time,' said Jo. 'This afternoon, we'll have our siesta—we'd have it, anyhow—and afterwards, go for a stroll through the forest to see the Pit, and then round the lake. And after *Kaffee*, we'd better pack up, I suppose. Then *Abendessen* early, and a long singsong. How's that, everybody?'

'O.K.!' declared Evadne.

'A very good idea, Jo,' said the captain. 'Have the day to remember as a typical one of this camp. Then that is decided. And as you've finished work, and I know some of you want to go to the village to buy souvenirs, we'll leave Miss Nalder, who has some letters to write, in charge, with Rufus as companion, and all go. So hurry up and get your clean overalls and scarves.'

They hurried, and when they were ready and formed in rank, they really looked a very smart company. There had been a proper wash-day on the Saturday before, and all had one set of clean garments which had been properly washed and ironed. Even the maltreated things of the Quintette's experiment had resumed something like their original appearance, though those young ladies had got heartily sick of rubbing and turning and beating before the whole of that corn-flour starch had been got out.

They marched down the white dusty road, and into the village, where they invaded the one shop in fours, and each came out with at least three parcels, which had to be tucked in safely when they got back to camp. Then came *Mittagessen;* and there they were upset to behold, not the fat, succulent-looking sausages they had expected, but heaps of frizzled sausage-meat.

'I can't think how it's happened, Madame,' wailed Vanna, who was head-cook that day. 'I'm sure we pricked them over and over again, just as you told us. But they all went pop like that!'

'Oh, it can't be helped,' said Miss Wilson, laughing. 'My dear girl, don't look so distressed. They will taste quite as good I expect. And sausages are like everything else—they have times of not doing the conventional thing expected of them.'

They certainly tasted delicious if the way they disappeared was anything by which to judge. They were followed by ripe plums and sponge-cake, the whole washed down by some of Grizel's delicious fruit drink. After that, while the heated cooks rested, the others cleared up, and the usual siesta followed. When it ended, they strolled off through the woods, laughing and chatting, till they came to Jo's pit.

'Remember how you spoke to Bill, Joey?' teased Juliet.

'Oh, be quiet!' said Jo hastily. 'If you come to that, remember how you fished up a dead body that wasn't?'

'What English from a future novelist!' said Miss Stewart. 'Well, we've seen that, so I suppose we had better go on.'

They insisted on going down the path to the tree where Elisaveta, Evadne, Maria, and Hilda had discovered the hornet's nest, and then they came back to camp, took to the boats, and sailed over that black patch where Juliet had hooked up the lay-figure.

'And we never caught a pike after all!' lamented Jo.

'I don't want to, thank you,' said Grizel, with a shudder. 'You saw that one the men caught last Wednesday. Ugh! What teeth!'

'I know. Still, it would have been rather jolly if we'd been able to say we *had* caught one,' persisted Jo.

'Tell you what, Joey,' put in Anne, a twinkle of mischief in her dark eyes, 'you dangle one foot in the water, and I'll bet a pike comes to see what it is. When it's got good hold, yell, and we'll pull you in.'

Jo was indignant at the suggestion, but she knew well enough that if she showed it, she would be teased for the rest of the day, so she held her peace. Luckily, Simone was in another boat, so she heard nothing of it, and therefore did not rush to the rescue, as she assuredly would have done otherwise. The girls, seeing that Jo had no intention of 'rising,' turned the boat, and rowed back to their own shore, where they set to work to get *Kaffee und Kuchen*, which they ate happily.

Packing was a sad task, for they had all enjoyed their fortnight, and it was hard to have to say good-bye to this jolly, care-free life. However, it had to be done, so they did it as quickly as they could. *Abendessen* followed and then, while the Roses washed up, the rest collected great piles of wood, and built up a huge fire for the last one. When everything was ready and the cups of cocoa had been handed round, they began their singsong with the time-honoured 'Camp-fire's Burning!' After this they sang nearly every song they knew, from 'Polly Wolly Doodle' to Parry's 'Jerusalem.' Joey was in great demand as usual, and sang beautifully Farrar's 'Knight of Bethlehem,' following it up with 'The Lark in the Morn.' Frieda and Marie sang together Schubert's 'Heiden Röslein,' and Cornelia lifted up her voice in the old negro spiritual, 'Were you there?' Finally, all standing together, they sang the national songs of each country represented in the camp, and wound up with 'Taps.'

The next morning was all hurry and scurry, for they were late in waking, and they must be ready when the charabancs and lorries came. But they managed it, and were presently striking the tents, gathering into a heap the stones which had formed their two fireplaces, making sure that no rubbish was left behind, and removing, as far as they could, all traces of their presence there. When, finally, there were only the paler rings on the grass, and the ashes rubbed into the bare ground to show where tents, fire, and incinerator had stood, they heaved up their packs; the men with the lorries shouldered the rest of the baggage; and the whole company filed off to the forest. At the edge, Joey, Frieda, Simone, Maria, Grizel, and Juliet stopped to look back.

'It has been a lovely time,' said Juliet. 'I hope that some day we may come back here.'

'So do I,' said Grizel.

Joey turned again, as the rest moved off. Lightly, she waved her hand to the still, silvery lake, gleaming in the September sunlight. 'Good-bye, little Baumersee!' she said softly. 'Till we meet again!' Then she ran after the others, whistling merrily.